HEROIC ADVENTURE AT ITS BEST

Stark was halfway up the steps.

There were blue robes in front of him, and on either side, and behind. They were absorbed in their chanting. Victims customarily went smiling to their deaths. Only at the very end, when they had been cast into the sea and the Children had begun to share them, were there cries amid the blood and the floating garlands.

The monks did not notice that Stark had ceased to smile.

He was still beyond any rational thought. He only knew that death was coming swiftly through the silken water to claim him.

Then, like a savage beast awakening, the life within him stirred!

"LEIGH BRACKETT COMBINES THE BEST OF A. MERRITT AND EDGAR RICE BURROUGHS WITH MUCH THAT IS UNIQUELY HER OWN!"

—Lester del Rey

THE
REAVERS
OF SKAITH

Volume Three of
The Book of Skaith

LEIGH BRACKETT

A Del Rey Book

BALLANTINE BOOKS • NEW YORK

A Del Rey Book
Published by Ballantine Books

Library of Congress Catalog Card Number: 76-7345

ISBN 0-345-28654-5

Manufactured in the United States of America

First Edition: August 1976
Second Printing: February 1980

First Canadian Printing: September 1976

Maps by Bob Porter

Cover art by James Steranko

To L. Sprague de Camp
and
Lin Carter:
Swordsmen and sorcerers
Sans peur et sans reproche

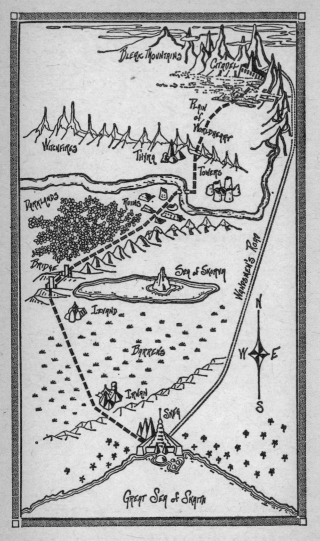

Stark's journey to the Citadel (*The Ginger Star*)

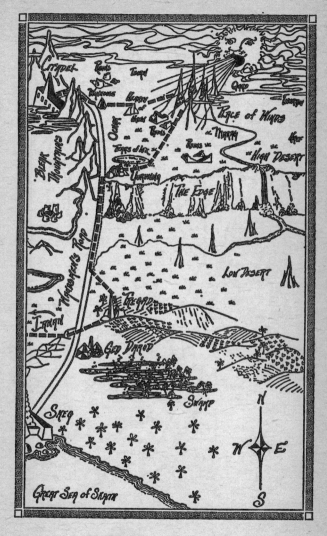

Stark's return to Irnan (*The Hounds of Skaith*)

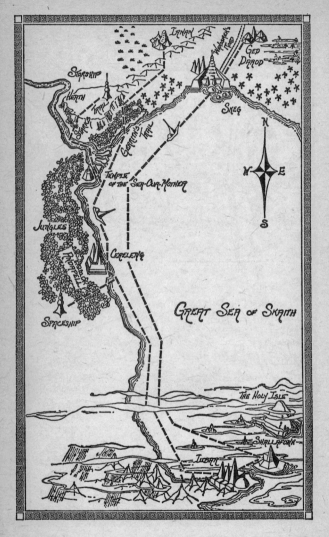

Stark's and Gerrith's journey to Iubar and return to
Ged Darod (*The Reavers of Skaith*)

THE BACKGROUND

SKAITH, dying planet of a dying star far out in the Orion Spur. Knowledge of the inevitable demise of their world has colored every facet of life for the people of Skaith, giving rise to many strange religions and customs. Over the centuries, different groups have sought salvation in different ways.

Some preferred, through controlled genetic mutation—a science now long lost—to worship a chosen deity with their whole being, as:

THE CHILDREN OF THE SEA-OUR-MOTHER, who have returned to the primal womb whence all life sprang, losing their humanity in the process, and with it their understanding of the coming doom;

THE CHILDREN OF SKAITH-OUR-MOTHER, who worship their equivalent of the Earth-Mother, dwelling deep within her warm, protective body, safe from the creeping death Outside;

THE FALLARIN, who wanted wings, the better to adore their dying lord, the Sun. In them, however, the mutation was imperfect—they have wings but cannot really fly. In compensation, they have become brothers to the winds, with power to call upon the currents of the air to do their bidding. They are served by

THE TARF, who are genetic mutations from non-human stock.

The above are relatively small groups. Most of the other survivors of the Wandering —that time of chaos when the great cities of the north were abandoned to the cold—have adapted to existing conditions and lead not-uncomfortable lives in the Fertile Belt, though strange survivals still exist in the Barrens and in the Darklands of the north (such as the Harsenyi, a tribe of northern nomads, message-bearers between various groups, and the Outdwellers, a strange far-northern people given to cannibalism). The productive section of the population has been harnessed to the support of the largest body of doom-worshipers.

THE FARERS, who, feeling that all effort is useless because there is no future for Skaith, spend their lives in faring from place to place as the mood takes them, filling their hours with the gratifications of the moment, secure in the knowledge that they will be fed, housed, clothed, and cared for by the authority of

THE WANDSMEN, whose rule brought stability out of chaos after the Wandering, but who, after two thousand years or so, have become onerous to many, as their original plan, which was to protect the weak from the strong, to feed the hungry, and to shelter the homeless, has become warped by time and the necessities of power into a serfdom under which the providers labor. The Wandsmen enforce their laws by the use of mercenary troops. The Wandsmen's superiors, or "officers," are

THE LORDS PROTECTOR, a council of seven old men drawn from the highest ranks of the Wandsmen, chosen for their wisdom and ability. These are regarded almost as deities by the Farers, and since their rule has been unbroken and their individual personalities always hidden from the vulgar gaze, they are thought to be immortal.

THE NORTHHOUNDS are genetically mutated animals bred as guardians of the Citadel. They are telepaths, and kill by destroying human minds with fear. Stark became their leader at the Citadel.

Skaith, in her heyday, despite advanced technology, scientific knowledge, and industrial might, never developed spaceflight, so that when she began her long dying, depleted of resources and her people slipping back into barbarism, there was no chance of escape for anyone—until the starships came. Then the poison of hope began to work, and the lines of battle were drawn between the entrenched power of the Wandsmen and the rebels who have demanded freedom to emigrate to a better world.

THE PLACES

THE CITADEL, a half-legendary retreat of the Lords Protector, in the High North. Destroyed by the off-worlder Stark.

GED DAROD, holy city of the Wandsmen, a place of pilgrimage, seat of their temporal power.

IRNAN, a city-state in the north temperate zone. Here Gerrith, the wise woman, made her prophecy of the Dark Man from the stars who would destroy the Lords Protector and set her people free. For this she was slain by the Wandsmen. The Irnanese were prime movers in the fight for emigration.

TREGAD, a similar city-state, sometime ally of Irnan.

SKEG, a seaport and formerly the location of the only star-port, until that was burned by order of the Wandsmen and the starships banished forever from Skaith.

YURUNNA, a northern base of the Wandsmen, where the Northhounds were bred. Captured by Stark with a coalition of desert tribesmen and Fallarin.

THYRA, a place south of and near the Witchfires, where a race of smiths reclaim iron from the rusting bones of a great ruined city.

THE TOWERS, another ruin, where the People of the Towers dwell in the northern cold and darkness, awaiting the coming of the starships.

IZVAND, a city by the Sea of Skorva in the Barrens. It is inhabited by a hardy people: fisherfolk and mercenary soldiers.

PAX, the hopefully named administrative center of the Galactic Union, a vast and far-flung confederation of worlds totally unknown to Skaith before the starships came. Pax is both a world and a city—a city so vast that it covers an entire planet. Pax contains closed-environment quarters to suit the needs of delegates, human and otherwise, from all the federated worlds; and it is to Pax that delegates must come from those *un*federated worlds, such as Skaith, which seek to join the Union.

THE PLACE OF WINDS, home of the Fallarin, isolated in the northern desert.

THE WITCHFIRES, a mountain range in the north, beneath which the Children of Skaith dwell in the House of the Mother.

THE THERMAL PITS, spoutings of underground hot water, south of the Bleak Mountains.

THE BLEAK MOUNTAINS, in the High North, location of the Wandsmen's Citadel.

THE PLAIN OF WORLDHEART, flat region south of the Thermal Pits and north of the Witchfires.

THE DARKLANDS, a danger-filled area north of Izvand and the Sea of Skorva and south of the Witchfires.

THE PEOPLE

ERIC JOHN STARK, called also N'Chaka, Man-Without-a-Tribe. A feral child reared by half-human aborigines in a cruel environment on the planet Mercury; in his mature years, a wanderer and mercenary specializing in the small wars of remote peoples fighting for survival against stronger opponents.

SIMON ASHTON, Stark's foster-father and friend, an official in the Ministry of Planetary Affairs at Pax. When Ashton disappeared on Skaith, Stark came to search for him.

YARROD, a martyr of Irnan, slain by the Wandsmen.

GERRITH, daughter of the slain Gerrith, who suc-
ceeded her as wise woman of Irnan.

HALK, Yarrod's companion-in-arms, an unwilling
ally of Stark.

BRECA, Halk's shield-mate, slain at Thyra.

ALDERYK, King of the Fallarin, companion of
Stark.

KLATLEKT, a Tarf, loyal servant-in-arms to Alderyk.

SABAK, leader of the desert tribesmen who followed Stark south.

TUCHVAR, former apprentice to the Houndmaster
of Yurunna, follower of Stark, devoted to his
hounds.

GERD and **GRITH,** Northhounds.

BAYA, a Farer girl who betrayed Stark and then
was captured by him. Freed by the Wandsmen, she again sought to destroy Stark at
Tregad.

FERDIAS, chief of the Lords Protector, Stark's bitter enemy.

GELMAR, Chief Wandsman of Skeg, a bitter enemy
also.

PEDRALLON, a Wandsman of high rank and prince
of Andapell, in the tropics. A champion of

emigration, he was punished as a traitor by his peers.

KELL À MARG, Skaith-Daughter, ruler of the Children of Skaith-Our-Mother.

THE IRONMASTER, ruler of the smiths of Thyra.

HARGOTH THE CORN-KING, ruler, with his sorcerer-priests, of the People of the Towers.

SANGHALAIN, Lady of Iubar, a principality in the White South.

MORN, leader of the Ssussminh, an amphibian race closely allied to the House of Iubar.

KAZIMNI OF IZVAND, a mercenary captain.

PENKAWR-CHE, a star-captain who made arrangements with Pedrallon and Stark to transport a delegation from Skaith to Pax in order to plead for membership in the Galactic Union. Penkawr-Che then betrayed his trust, held his passengers to ransom, and in company with two other ships has seized the opportunity to loot Skaith.

1

Strong bindings held N'Chaka fast to the flat, hard surface whereon he lay.

There was too much light above him. He could barely make out the face that leaned and looked down into his own. It moved and pulsed and swam with the movement of his blood, a handsome face cut from burnished gold, with a crest of hair like curled wires. There were other faces, dim in the shadows at the sides, but only that one mattered. He could not remember whose face it was. Only that it mattered.

There was pain again, the hollow jab of a needle. N'Chaka snarled, and fought the straps.

The golden face asked a question.

N'Chaka heard. He did not wish to answer, but he had no choice. The poison running in him forced him to answer.

He spoke, in the clicks and grunts of a language so primitive that it was only a little more complex than the speech of apes.

Penkawr-Che, the golden man, said, "He reverts to that every time. Interesting. Bring Ashton."

Ashton was brought.

The question was repeated, and the answer.

"You're his foster-father. Do you know what language he is speaking?"

"The aboriginals of Sol One speak that tongue. He was reared by them after his own parents were killed. Until he came into my care—at fourteen, or thereabouts—that was the only speech he knew."

1

"Can you translate?"

"I was one of the administrators of Sol One. Part of my duty was to protect the abos from the miners. I wasn't always successful. But I knew them well." He translated meticulously, and smiled. "There are no words in that vocabulary for the things you want to know about."

"Ah," said Penkawr-Che. "Well, then. Let me think."

2

The million little bells of Ged Darod chimed softly from the roofs and spires of the Lower City, where the warm wind rocked them. It was a cheerful sound, speaking of love and kindness. But in the packed streets—among the temples to Old Sun, to Skaith-Mother and Sea-Mother, and to my lord Darkness and his lady Cold and their daughter Hunger, the deadly trinity who already possessed almost half the planet—the people were silent and dismayed.

The temples held many suppliants, asking the gods to protect their own; but the larger portion of the crowd looked elsewhere. Farers in the thousands filled the parks and the pleasure gardens; made up of all the races of the Fertile Belt, dressed, painted, and adorned in every conceivable manner, these free, careless, and perpetually itinerant children of the Lords Protector—who saw, through their servants, the Wandsmen, that the hungry were always fed and the needy succored—turned their faces to the Upper City. The Wandsmen had never failed them. Surely they would somehow manage to turn aside the alien menace that still threatened them from out the sky, even after the burning of the starport.

One ship had gone from Skaith carrying traitors who wished to overturn the rule of the Wandsmen and replace it with that of a foreign power. If this should be accomplished, the Farers knew that they, and the way of life that sustained them, would be swept away.

They milled in the vast square below the Wandsmen's Gate and waited in the hope of salvation.

High in the Upper City, which housed the heart and center of the Wandsmen's power, the Lord Protector Ferdias stood at a window in the Palace of the Twelve, looking down at the splendor of flashing domes and glittering peacock tiles. Ferdias was an old man, but age had not bowed his unyielding back nor dimmed the harsh fire of his eye. He wore the white robes of his rank, and not the slightest shadow of humility betrayed the fact that Ferdias had come back to Ged Darod as a fugitive.

Yet he was keenly aware of that fact. Very keenly. Especially upon this day.

A massive door opened somewhere behind him. Voices sounded, subdued and distant in the cavernous room. Ferdias remained as he was. There was no longer any urgency.

He had begun his life of service as a gray apprentice within these mighty walls. He had not known then that Old Sun, the ginger star that ruled his heaven, had been recorded as a number on the galactic charts of a civilization he had never heard of. He had not known that he dwelt, along with his sun and his planet, in a remote sector of something these people had named the Orion Spur. He had not known that the galaxy, out beyond his lonely little sky, contained a vast and busy complex of worlds and men known as the Galactic Union.

How happy he had been without that knowledge! How happy he would have remained had it never been vouchsafed him. But knowledge had dropped unbidden, in flame and thunder, out of the clouds, and innocence was forever lost.

In a little more than a dozen years, the starships had brought many benefits to the sad old world of Ferdias' birth, starved for the metals and minerals it no longer possessed. So the foreign men had been allowed to come and go, carefully watched and supervised, from the single starport at Skeg. But the ships had brought less welcome things: heresies, treasons, rebellions, war—and, at the end, a mad stranger out of the stars, who had set the all-powerful Lords Protector fleeing down the roads of Skaith away from their burning rooftree, homeless as any Farers.

Ferdias set his hands on the massive stone of the windowsill and felt the solidity of it. He smiled. He saw the light of Old Sun shining upon the streets below, upon the mass of humanity that waited there, and his heart opened with a physical pang, sending a flooding warmth throughout his body so that he caught his breath and his sight became blurred with tears. These were his people, to whose welfare he had devoted his life—the poor, the weak, the homeless, the hungry. His children, his beloved children.

Because of my error, he said to them in the silence of his mind, *you were almost destroyed. But the gods of Skaith have not forsaken you.* And, he added humbly, *Nor me.*

In the room behind him, someone coughed. It was neither a hastening nor an impatient cough.

Ferdias sighed and turned.

"My lord Gorrel," he said, "get you back to your bed. You have no business here."

"No," said Gorrel, and shook his gaunt old head. "I shall remain."

He sat in a large chair that was a cocoon of wrappings and cushions; he had not yet recovered from the journey south. Ferdias thought that Gorrel was not likely to recover, and that it was less the hardships of travel than the shattering shock of what had happened at the Citadel that had broken Gorrel's health.

"Well, then," he said gently, "perhaps you may find fresh strength in what I have to tell you."

Besides Gorrel, in the room now stood five other old men in the same white robes that Ferdias wore, making up the seven Lords Protector. Behind them were the Twelve, the council of senior Wandsmen in tunics of somber red, with gold-tipped wands of office in their hands. Standing a little apart from the Twelve was another red-clad Wandsman, on whose proud and bitter face Ferdias' gaze rested for a long moment.

"This has been a cruel time," Ferdias began, "a time of tribulation, when it seemed as if the very fabric of our society was being rent. Tregad joined the revolt against us, and we suffered a crushing defeat at Irnan. We were betrayed, here at Ged Darod, by one of our own, the Wandsman Pedrallon, who caused a starship to land in defiance of our decree and take on passengers—men and women, including Pedrallon himself, who wished to deliver Holy Mother Skaith to the Galactic Union as a member planet, thus putting an end to our rule. It has been a time when we could foresee the destruction of twenty centuries of work and devotion in the service of mankind, a service which has endured since the Wandering."

He paused, aware of their intent faces all turned toward him. He smiled again, with a kind of ferocious benevolence.

"I have called you together here," he said, "to tell you that that time has ended."

Out of the sudden shocked confusion of voices, one rose strong and clear, the voice of an orator. It was Jal Bartha, who would not be chosen from among the Twelve to take old Gorrel's place among the Lords Protector when it fell vacant, though Ferdias knew that he hoped to be. Jal Bartha's lack of judgment might have been borne, but his conceit never.

"How can that be, my lord?" Jal Bartha demanded. "These traitors you speak of are well on their way to Pax, the man Stark moves among the city-states preaching the gospel of starflight, our Wandsmen are driven out or slain—"

"If your silver tongue can be stilled for a moment," said Ferdias quietly, "I shall make all things clear."

Jal Bartha flushed, and inclined his head stiffly.

Ferdias glanced once again at the thirteenth Wandsman, and clapped his hands.

A small door opened at the side of the great chamber.

Two men in green tunics entered, with a third between them. He wore blue, marking his lesser rank, and he was young and utterly distressed.

"This man's name is Llandric," said Ferdias. "One of Pedrallon's creatures, a small serpent in our midst. He has something to say to you."

Llandric stammered.

Ferdias commanded, on a note of chilled steel, "Say it, Llandric, as you said it to me."

"Yes," he began, "I—I serve Pedrallon." He seemed to find his courage, facing their hostility with a sort of quiet defiance. "I believe that the peoples of Skaith must be free to emigrate, if only for one reason —that the planet's livable areas grow smaller each year and room must be made."

'We do not require a lecture on Pedrallon's heresies," said Jal Bartha. "We understand them well enough."

"I don't think you understand them at all," said Llandric, "but that's beside the point. After Pedrallon went away, we have continued to monitor the transceiver which he secured from the Antarean, Penkawr-Che, and which was Pedrallon's secret means of communication with the off-worlders. Because of that monitoring, I am able to tell you what has happened, and that is why I am here. I myself have heard the talking of the starships."

The thirteenth Wandsman stepped forward. "What starships? I drove them all from Skeg, with the flames of the burning behind them. What starships?"

"There are three," said Llandric. "One is the ship of Penkawr-Che, the off-worlder who agreed with Pedrallon and the man Stark to take our delegations to Galactic Center, at Pax. Penkawr-Che has betrayed us. He has not gone to Pax. He has returned to Skaith with the two other ships in company, and all his passengers."

Ferdias quelled the outburst that followed. "My lords, please! Let him continue."

"I first knew of this," Llandric said, "when word

was brought to me that three ships had met in orbit above Skaith. I went at once to the hidden place where the transceiver is kept and listened, myself. Penkawr-Che had transferred three of his passengers —Pedrallon into one ship, Lady Sanghalain of Iubar and the person Morn into the other. This latter ship was to land at Iubar in the far south and demand payment for the Lady. The other ship was to go to Andapell, Pedrallon's country, where he is a prince and would bring a high ransom. Penkawr-Che himself was to land at Tregad and sell them back their elders, and then at Irnan for the same purpose. That has been done."

There was a silence in the room—the silence of men digesting unlooked-for news, sucking the juices from it, tasting to see if it be truth.

The thirteenth Wandsman spoke in a strange dry voice. "Irnan, you said."

"Yes."

"The man Stark was at Irnan. What of him?"

"Tell them," said Ferdias. "They are much interested in the man Stark."

"Penkawr-Che demanded Stark as part of the ransom. He has knowledge of some treasure in the High North that Penkawr-Che wants. The Antarean also took back the flying thing that he had left with Stark."

The thirteenth Wandsman reached out and grasped Llandric's tunic at the throat. "Speak plainly," he said. "To demand is not necessarily to receive. What of the man Stark?"

"He is taken. He is Penkawr-Che's prisoner."

"Taken!"

The Lords Protector savored that word. Lord Gorrel repeated it several times, rolling it between his skeletal jaws.

"Taken," said the thirteenth Wandsman, "but not dead."

"The last talk I heard between the ships was last night. Iubar had paid Sanghalain's ransom; Pedrallon had been redeemed in Andapell. They spoke about the temples and other places they would loot. Penkawr-Che had landed at a place the other captains knew of, and would begin to plunder the *tlun* villages in the jungles between the uplands and the sea. He was questioning Stark, he said, and hoped for results soon. Then he said he would kill both the Earthmen, though there was small chance they could ever testify about what the star-captains had done."

Llandric shook his head angrily. "Stark is neither here nor there. These outlaw captains have come to rob and kill our people. That is why I made the decision to give myself up to you, so that you would know all this while there was yet time to stop them. And they must be stopped!"

His voice had risen until he was all but shouting.

"I know where some of them are," Llandric continued. "Where some of them intend to strike. They don't know that they were overheard. I didn't speak to them. It would have been useless, and I was afraid they might send one of the flying things to destroy the transceiver. But the ships are at rest now, while the flying things do the raiding, and if you move swiftly . . ."

Ferdias said, "Enough, Llandric. My lords, you see how matters have turned out for us, how well Mother Skaith guards her own. The traitors have been made to pay for their folly. The man Stark is a prisoner and will die, along with Ashton. All the dangers that threatened us are swept away at a single stroke by one man's action. Shall we grudge that man his just reward?"

There was noise enough in the room then, voices raised all at cross purposes like the sharp waves in a riptide.

Llandric stared at Ferdias, not believing. "I thought perhaps Pedrallon was mistaken about you. I thought perhaps you honestly did not see where your policies were leading. But this is not a matter of opinion, this is fact. This is murder. And you speak of reward?"

"My young fool," said Ferdias, not unkindly, "*your* people brought this scourge about, not *we*. Do not expect us to relieve you of your guilt." He held up his hands. "Please, my lords! Let us be tranquil and apply our minds."

He moved back to the window, where he could see the flash of Old Sun's light on the golden domes and hear the chiming of the bells.

"Because of us, our world was able to survive the chaos of the Wandering and reshape itself into a new and stable order that has endured for centuries and that will continue to endure as long as we control the forces of disruption. With the passing of the opportunity to escape by starship, those forces would seem to be controlled, since the disaffected no longer have any hope of evading their responsibilities.

"But can we be sure that the threat will not come again? Other starships may seek us out as the earlier ones did. Other folk may be tempted as the people of Irnan were tempted."

He paused, and the others waited: his six white-robed colleagues; the Twelve in red, with their gold-tipped wands; the thirteenth Wandsman with the bitter face; Llandric between his guards.

Ferdias said, "I wish this lesson to be so well learned that it will never be forgotten. I wish the name of *foreigner* to be anathema. I wish the people of Skaith to learn, in pain and terror, to hate everything that may come to them from beyond the sky. I wish no one ever again to desire foreign rule."

He looked down upon the crowded streets of the Lower City. "A few innocents will suffer, and that is to be regretted. But it is for the good of all. My lords, are we in agreement that no steps shall be taken against these star-captains?"

Only Jal Bartha raised a question.

"The depredations may not be so harsh or so widespread as to cause such a feeling among the people."

"Great trees need only little seeds to spring from. We shall see to it that the news travels." Ferdias went and stood in front of Llandric. "Do you under-stand now?"

"I understand that I've offered up my life for nothing." Llandric's young face had taken on a totally unfamiliar sternness. It seemed to have aged ten years. "This is how you do good. You allow your children—the children you claim to love so dearly—to be slaughtered out-of-hand as a cold matter of policy."

"That is why you could never be a Lord Protector," said Ferdias. "You have not the long view." He shrugged. "Not many will be slaughtered, after all. And in any case, how could we hope to stand against the weapons of these foreigners?"

Llandric said cruelly, "You are an old man, Ferdias, and your long view is all of the past. When the starving hordes close in on you from north and south, and there is no escape for anyone, remember who it was that barred the roads of space."

The guards took him out.

Ferdias spoke to the thirteenth Wandsman.

"A day of triumph, Gelmar, after long adversity. I wished you to share it."

Gelmar, Chief Wandsman of Skeg, looked at him with a dark glitter in his eyes. "I am grateful, my lord. I shall make thank-offerings to all the gods that the man Stark is taken." He paused, and then added with savage anger, "It does not change the fact that it was my task to take him, and I failed."

"We all failed, Gelmar. Remember that it was by my order that Simon Ashton was made captive and brought to me at the Citadel. But for that, Stark would never have come to Skaith to find him; there would have been no prophecy of Irnan; there prob-ably would have been no revolt; and the Citadel would not have been destroyed." Ferdias dropped a hand on Gelmar's arm. "It is over now. Even these last ships will soon be gone. Nothing has occurred that cannot be undone. We must begin to think now of rebuilding."

Gelmar nodded. "True, my lord. But I will not be satisfied until I know that Stark is dead."

3

N'Chaka was in a cage.

Cliffs rose up on either side of the narrow valley, stretching into black pinnacles that pierced the sky. The green place where the water bubbled was close by. His mouth was parched and his tongue a dry twig.

He could see the dark bodies on the green. The fresh red brightness of blood was turning black and ugly. Old One was dead, with all his tribe. The hammering echoes of killing still rang in N'Chaka's ears.

He howled and tore at the bars in rage and grief.

Someone spoke. "N'Chaka."

Man-Without-a-Tribe. His name. He had another one, he thought, but that was his true name.

"N'Chaka."

Father voice. Not Old One father. Simon father.

N'Chaka held the bars and remained still. His eyes were open, but darkness still poured across them, flickering with terrible pictures that were of a glaring brilliance. Heat and hairy corpses, the smell of blood on furnace air, snouted muzzles hideously smiling. He thought, *But my people never smiled.*

"Eric," said the father voice. "Eric John Stark. Look at me."

He tried. He could see nothing but the flickering of dark-bright images.

"Eric. N'Chaka. See."

Slowly, far away at the end of a long, hollow black-

13

ness, something took form. It began to come closer.
It rushed toward N'Chaka, or perhaps he fell toward
it, with a cold tearing sound that was felt rather than
heard, or heard with the raw nerves rather than the
ears. The darkness fell away, hissing like baffled surf,
and Simon Ashton was there on the other side of the
bars.

N'Chaka shivered. The images had gone. He no
longer saw the valley, the bubbling spring, the scattered bodies of his foster-folk. The men with the sharp
things had gone, too; they were no longer tormenting
him. But the bars had not gone.

"Take them," he said.

Simon Ashton shook his head. "I can't, Eric. I did
before, but that was a long time ago. You've been
drugged. Be patient. Wait till it clears."

N'Chaka fought the bars for a little while. Then he
was quiet. And gradually he saw that Simon Ashton
was bound, hand and foot, to a simple metal framework in the shape of an X, suspended by a rope from
the limb of a tall tree, and that he was quite naked.
So was the tree, devoid of leaves and bark, the exposed wood smooth and white as bone. The end of
the rope was belayed around the trunk.

Stark did not understand, but he sensed that understanding would come if he waited. Ashton's framework
swung slowly in the breeze, so that sometimes he was
facing Stark and sometimes he was not.

Beyond the tree stretched a great emptiness, a
blasted heath set with clumps of twisted thorn and
here and there a flayed trunk with skeletal branches,
and in between them a coarse growth of stunted grass
starred with little flowers. The flowers were white with
round, dark centers. They resembled watching eyes,
countless thousands of eyes, peering from side to side
as the breeze moved them.

It was late. Old Sun hung low in the west and the
shadows were long.

Stark turned and looked the other way.

A ship stood on the level plain, a tall needle shape raking the sky. Stark knew that ship.

Arkeshti.

Penkawr-Che.

The last of the drug-mist lifted from Stark's mind. Just so had *Arkeshti* stood before Irnan.

The blow had fallen so swiftly out of the dim sky. One moment all was well; and in the next moment— a shattering thunderbolt of sound and flame and fountaining dust—*Arkeshti* landed and the full extent of Penkawr-Che's betrayal became known.

Stark had remained at Irnan, of his own choice, to help protect the city against any threats from the Wandsmen that might arise before the Galactic Union representatives came. Faced with *Arkeshti* and her three armed hoppers, there had been nothing he could do. His own planet-hopper, obtained from Penkawr-Che when they were allies at the rescue of Irnan, and identical with the other three, possessed a laser cannon, powerful armament against the primitive weaponry of a planet long lost to the uses of advanced technology but worthless against adversaries such as these. *Arkeshti*'s impervious skin would shed the beam of the light cannon as it shed dust, and he could not hope to shoot down three skilled pilots before he himself was downed.

Even if he had wished to try, he had the hostages to think of.

There was Ashton. There was Jerann and the rest of Irnan's council of elders, and two of Alderyk's winged Fallarin, who had chosen to go to Pax as observers, all in Penkawr-Che's hands.

Only the radio in Stark's hopper had been used, to relay messages back and forth between the ship and the acting council of Irnan. For most of the time, the hostages had been held in full view of the city, in the open, under threat of death. Ashton had been with them, to ensure Stark's cooperation; Penkawr-Che had learned all he needed to know about that relationship.

Penkawr-Che also knew the exact sum that remained in Irnan's coffers.

Irnan paid. And part of the ransom demanded was Stark himself.

He had done his best to bargain for Ashton's freedom, but to no avail. Irnan's mood of savage anger and despair had given him no help.

He did not blame them. The Irnanese had endured months of siege by the mercenary troops of the Wandsmen. They had endured starvation and pestilence and the destruction of their rich valley. They had endured because they had hope—hope that all the suffering would lead to a better life on a new world, free of the oppressive rule of the Wandsmen and the burden of their army of Farer dependents, which grew larger with each generation. Now that hope was gone, shattered in a few brief moments by the treachery of an off-worlder. It would not come again in their lifetime. Perhaps it would never come again.

Meglin, who had headed the acting council in Jerann's absence, had looked at Stark bleakly and said, "The Wandsmen will come back now, and the Farers, and we shall be punished. Whether or not it was a crime, we were foolish indeed to put our trust in off-world men and foreign ways. We will have no more of them here." She had nodded toward the ship. "They are your people. Go."

He went. There was nothing else to do. Penkawr-Che had made it clear to him what would happen if he attempted to escape. Since not only Ashton but the elders were involved, the people of Irnan were making sure that he did not.

He had walked out alone to the starship. The Northhounds were of no use to him now. His comrades were of no use. He left them behind, all those who had come south with him to help raise the siege of Irnan: the boy Tuchvar, with the hounds; the company of Hooded Men from the northern deserts; the dark-winged, dark-furred Fallarin, brothers to the wind, who had stripped themselves of their golden torques and girdles to pay the ransom for their fellows.

He left Irnan behind. It was like walking away from the corpse of someone who has been for a time vitally important in one's life, and who has suddenly died.

He also left behind the wise woman Gerrith, and that was like leaving a part of himself.

They had had so little time to talk.

"You must not be here when the Wandsmen come," he told her, because that thought was most urgent in his mind. "They'll do to you as they did to your mother."

Halk, the tall swordsman who had fought beside them both across half of Skaith, said cruelly, "We can all find safety somewhere, Dark Man, so don't concern yourself with us. Worry about yourself. You know your people better than I do, but I think Penkawr-Che means you no good."

Gerrith touched him, once, with the tips of her fingers. "I'm sorry, Stark. I did not foresee. If I had only been able to give you warning—"

"It would have made no difference," Stark said. "He has Ashton."

And they had parted, without even a moment alone to say goodbye.

Stark had passed the hostage elders, who looked at him with cold, stunned hatred—not because he himself had committed any wrong, but because they had built such hopes upon him, the Dark Man of the prophecy, who would bring them freedom. Only old Jerann spoke to him.

"We set our feet on this road together," he said. "It has been an ill road for both of us."

Stark had not answered him. He walked on to where Ashton stood between his guards, and they entered the ship together.

That had been . . . when? He could not remember.

He looked again at Ashton, hanged man on a dangling frame.

"How long?"

"You were taken yesterday."

"Where are we? How far from Irnan?"

"Very far. West and south. Too far to think of going back, even if you were free. Your friends will all be gone from there before another sun."

"Yes," said Stark, and wondered if the chance would ever come to him to kill Penkawr-Che.

The cage was not tall enough to allow Stark to stand up. He went round it on all fours, as naked as Ashton. He had nothing he could use as a weapon, not so much as a pebble. The cage had no door. He had been put into it drugged, and the remaining bars had been welded in place afterward. He tested each bar in turn. They seemed stout enough to hold him.

He fought down a surge of claustrophobia and spoke once more to Ashton.

"I remember Penkawr-Che questioning me, and I remember the needles. Did I tell him what he wanted to know?"

"You told him. But you told him in your natal tongue. He made me translate for him—only the hairy abos hadn't any words to express the things he wanted to know. So he decided that drugging you was a waste of time."

"I see," said Stark. "He's going to use you, instead. Has he hurt you?"

"Not yet."

Two hoppers came drumming in on their sturdy rotors and settled down by the ship, near two others that must have come in earlier. Men got out and began unloading cylindrical packages wrapped in coarse fiber: *tlun*, a mind-expanding drug, immensely valuable in foreign markets.

"They've begun raiding into the jungle," Ashton said. "The day seems to have been profitable."

Stark was thinking of other things. "At least we have another chance."

Ashton's metal frame revolved at the end of the

rope. "I don't think he's going to let us live, in any case. If, by some remote and impossible chance, one of us should get back to civilization, it would mean the end of him."

"I know," said Stark. "It wasn't love of the Children of Skaith-Our-Mother that kept me from talking."

He tested the bars again.

A yellow bird had appeared, walking through the coarse grass. The eye-flowers watched it. It came and stood beneath the tree where Ashton hung. It looked up at him, moving its head back and forth as the frame moved. It was a largish bird, about two feet high, with very strong legs. It appeared to be flightless. Presently it began to climb the trunk of the tree, striking its claws into the dead wood with a clearly audible clicking.

Both men watched it. It climbed steadily to the branch from which Ashton was suspended. It walked out along the branch to a position above Ashton's head and stood peering earnestly down at him. Its beak was black, polished and shiny, and sharply curved and pointed.

Ashton's head was bent back. He stared upward, at the bird.

It gave a happy gurgling cry and dropped from the branch.

Stark and Ashton both shouted at the same instant. Ashton made a convulsive movement that set the frame swinging. The bird clutched at him, missed its grip, and continued to drop, thrashing its small wings and squawking angrily. It struck the ground with a thump and sat there.

Ashton looked at the red lines where the claws had raked him. Stark was concentrating with single-minded purpose on one of the bars, trying to force it.

The bird picked itself up, settled its feathers, and began once more to climb the trunk of the tree.

Someone threw a stone at it. It squawked again and

jumped away into the grass, where it scuttled off with amazing speed.

Penkawr-Che walked up and stood, smiling, between Ashton and the cage.

4

The Antarean was tall, and he moved with a jaunty, loose-limbed stride like a lion carelessly at ease. His skin was a clear golden color, drawn smoothly over strong, high-arching bones. His eyes were a darker gold, and the pupils were slitted. His close-curled hair was like a cap, snug against his broad skull. He wore a very rich tunic of smoke-gray silken stuff over tight black trousers. In his right hand he carried a whip with a long, thin lash. At the end of the lash, jingling lightly together, were several small metallic objects like the jointed tails of scorpions.

"In spite of its unpleasant appearance," said Pen-kawr-Che, "this upland does support something of a population. The tenacity of life is always amazing. One wonders. What does the yellow bird live on, apart from odd finds like Ashton? Why does it want to live at all, in these surroundings? I can't tell you. But it will be back, probably with its mate. In the meantime, you two have other problems."

He looked from Stark to Ashton, and back again to Stark.

"You will answer my questions this time, unless for some reason you are more attached to the Children of Skaith, who tried to kill you, than you are to this man, who fostered you."

Almost without looking, he flicked the scorpion-tail lash of the whip at Ashton's body. There came a short sharp cry, quickly silenced.

"Ashton is more communicative than you are under

drugs. I already know enough from him to find the Witchfires, since he actually saw them when he was a prisoner in the north. But he was never inside the House of the Mother and so was only able to repeat to me what you had told him. Now, is it true that this vast complex of caverns under the Witchfires is a storehouse for artifacts from the past of this planet?"

"That is true," said Stark. "The Children have a passion for history. I suppose it has kept them from going completely mad since they left the outer world behind them." He looked at Penkawr-Che through the bars, then at Ashton's bleeding body pendant from the tree. "You could fill the holds of three ships, and three again, with the things in those caverns; and each piece would be worth a fortune in the collectors' market."

"So I thought," said Penkawr-Che. "Describe to me the entrance to the caverns from the pass of the Witchfires, and the defenses there. Describe the North Gate, by which you escaped. Tell me how many men this Kell à Marg, Skaith-Daughter, can set against me, how they're armed, what kind of fighters they are."

Stark said, "Something for nothing is no bargain, Penkawr-Che. And I don't talk well in cages."

Again the lash flicked out.

"Do you wish to torture Ashton, or do you wish to get the information?" Stark asked.

Penkawr-Che considered, drawing the long, thin lash through his fingers. "Supposing I let you out of the cage. What then?"

"Ashton comes down from there."

"Then what?"

"Let us go that far," said Stark, "and then see."

Penkawr-Che laughed. He clapped his hands. Four men emerged from the litter of the semi-camp which had sprouted overnight beside the base of the ship. At Penkawr-Che's order, they tailed onto the rope and lowered Ashton to the ground, unbinding him and helping him to stand.

"There is half your bargain," said Penkawr-Che.

Each of the four men had a stunner holstered at his belt. Two of them, in addition, carried long-range weapons slung across their backs.

Old Sun slid wearily toward the horizon. Shadows flowed together across the heath.

Stark shrugged. "The northern gate opens onto the Plain of Worldheart. There is a guardroom immediately inside, and beyond that a corridor protected by slabs of stone which can be let down to form a series of barriers. The gate itself is a slab of stone which moves on pivots. You might search for a hundred years along that face of the Witchfires and never find it." He smiled at Penkawr-Che. "There is a third of your bargain."

Penkawr-Che said, "Continue."

"Not till I'm free of these bars."

The lash flicked. Ashton's eyes filled with tears, but he did not cry out.

Stark said brutally, "Flay him if you will. Until I'm free of this cage, you get nothing more."

In a stiff, flat voice Ashton said, "If you push him too far, Penkawr-Che, you will get nothing at any time. He reverts easily."

Penkawr-Che studied Stark. He saw a man, big and dark and powerful, scarred with old battles. A mercenary, with a life spent in the small primitive wars of small peoples on remote worlds. A dangerous man. This, Penkawr-Che knew and understood. But there was something about the eyes, disconcertingly light and clear. They had a kind of blaze in them, something at once innocent and deadly—a beast's eyes, startling to see in a human face.

Ashton added, "He cannot endure being caged."

Penkawr-Che spoke to one of the men, who went away and presently returned with a cutting torch. Removing one bar, he created a gap through which Stark might leave the cage but not in any swift dramatic leap. As he levered himself out, the men stood with their stunners in their hands, watching.

"Very well," said Penkawr-Che. "Now you are free."

Stark drew a long breath and shivered slightly, as an animal twitches its skin. He stood straight beside the cage.

"In the pass of the Witchfires," he said, "just below the crest, there is a rock formation called the Leaning Man. A gateway into the caverns lies close beneath him. It, too, is a pivoted slab of stone. Inside is a large cavern where the Harsenyi nomads come to trade with the Children. A second door leads into the House of the Mother. Beyond this door is a long corridor, guarded by barriers as the North Gate is guarded, but by more of them—and stronger. No invader has ever breached those defenses."

"I have explosives."

"If you use them, the passage will be blocked by its own collapse."

"You give me small comfort," said Penkawr-Che. "What of the fighting men?"

"Both sexes bear arms." Stark was not sure of that, but no matter. "There will be four thousand at least, perhaps five or six. I can only make a guess. During most of the short time I was there, I was lost and wandering in total darkness. Much of the Mother's House has been abandoned, and there are obviously fewer of the Children than when it was constructed. But they are by no means extinct. They have no modern weapons, but they are stout fighters with what they have." Actually, he knew that they were not. "More important, they'll have the advantage of the ground. You'd have to take the chambers one by one, and you'd never come to the end of them."

"I have lasers."

"They will hide from them. The place is a maze. Even if you were able to force an entrance, they could keep you surrounded, attack unseen from every direction, pick you off one at a time. You would not have enough replacements."

Penkawr-Che frowned, drawing the lash again and again through his fingers.

Rusty twilight crept over the heath. Lights began to come on in the camp.

Penkawr-Che flicked the lash suddenly to draw blood from Stark's shoulder. "Your knowledge has proven to be of no value after all. We've both wasted our time." He turned, impatiently, to speak to his men.

"Wait," said Stark.

Penkawr-Che looked at him, squinting in the dusk. "Why should I wait?"

"Because I know a way into the House of Skaith-Mother that even her Children have forgotten."

"Ah!" said Penkawr-Che. "And how would you have happened to find that on your one brief visit, during most of which you wandered in the dark?"

"In the midst of darkness," Stark said, "I saw light. I will sell you this information."

"At what price?"

"Freedom."

Penkawr-Che's face was a mask, dim and obscure. After a while, so that he would not seem to be too eager, he nodded. "You're worth nothing to me dead. If I'm satisfied with your information, I'll take you and Ashton to wherever you wish, within reason—on Skaith, of course—and release you there."

"No," said Stark. "Release us here and now."

"It has to be my way."

"You'll get what you want *my* way or not at all. Think, Penkawr-Che. All those caverns crammed with treasures, and nothing to stop you—not a single barrier, not a single warrior with a spear. If you intend to let us go, what difference does it make to you where or how?"

"The heath is not a friendly-seeming place."

Stark laughed.

"All right," Penkawr-Che said impatiently. "If I'm satisfied, you may go free here and now."

"Good. I want clothing and weapons, and something for Ashton's wounds."

Penkawr-Che glowered, but he moved apart with one of his men, who presently hurried away.

The man returned quickly with a battery-powered lamp that he set on a packing case. Stark blessed it silently but tried not to look at it. The heath was quite dark now and would remain so until the first of the Three Ladies rose, perhaps a space of thirty minutes.

Ashton stood quietly. The harsh glare accentuated the leanness of his body, his bones seeming more prominent, his corded muscles more like wire ropes. Blood trickled in dark streams on the whiteness of his skin. He, too, had averted his face from the lamp. But he watched Stark.

Presently other men came with clothing. One of them treated Ashton with rough efficiency from a first-aid kit and then dabbed at the cut on Stark's shoulder. The two men dressed themselves in trousers and tunics and soft boots; the tunics were pale in color, and Stark was sorry for that.

"The weapons?"

Penkawr-Che shook his head. "Later, when I've heard what you have to say."

Stark had expected this. "All right," he said, "but Ashton goes now."

Penkawr-Che stared at him. "Why?"

"Why not, unless you're lying to me? Let's just call it a token of your good faith."

Penkawr-Che swore, but he nodded his head at Ashton. "Go, then."

He was confident. He held all the winning cards. He felt that he could afford to humor Stark. Besides, Ashton could not go far.

Ashton hesitated, then went away, out onto the dark heath.

Penkawr-Che said, "Talk."

Stark never lost sight of Ashton's faintly glimmering tunic.

"As I said, the Children are not as numerous as they were in the beginning. They are a controlled mutation, with no choice but to interbreed. Much of the Great House has been abandoned for generations, and I wandered in the black dark there for days, trying to find a way out."

"And then you saw the light."

"Yes. It came through an opening in the rock. There was a balcony at the opening, high up on the cliff. A lookout post, I imagine. Probably there are others. I was not able to climb down from it, so it did not help me to escape. But it's a doorway into the catacombs, unguarded, forgotten—"

"Inaccessible?"

"To any enemy that the Children were aware of when they built it. Not to you. Hoppers could ferry men up there. You could put an army inside with not a single blow struck. You might even manage to fill all your holds before the Children even knew what you were about."

Penkawr-Che looked at Stark narrow-eyed, as if he were trying to pierce his brain and pick out the truth.

"How would I find this balcony?"

"Bring me something to draw on. I'll make you a map."

Out on the heath, Ashton had reached a clump of thorn. He paused, looking back.

A sheet of thin plastic and a stylus were brought to Stark. He put the plastic on the packing case, beside the lamp. Penkawr-Che leaned over to watch. The four men stood around at a little distance, their stunners ready. Ashton meanwhile blended imperceptibly into the shadows of the thorn-trees and disappeared.

"See here," said Stark. "Here is the north face of the Witchfire, here the Plain of Worldheart, here the range of the Bleak Mountains, the Thermal Pits, the Citadel—what's left of it. Over here, to the west, the Harsenyi road that led to their camp. That is what I saw from the balcony. I took rough bearings."

"Which you were able to do without instruments."

"I'm a mercenary by trade, you know that. I have a trained eye." He held the stylus, rolling it between his fingers. "I can pinpoint the area for you so that your search will not take you more than half a day, using the hoppers."

"But," said Penkawr-Che, "at the moment you do not intend to do so."

"No. And if I do not give you the bearings, your search will take much more time. Longer, I think, than you will care to spend."

"You're a hard man to deal with, Stark. What is it you want now?"

"Tell your men to take their weapons and go away."

"That is quite impossible."

"I don't trust you. I don't want those men where they can drop me the moment I finish the map."

"You have my word that they won't." Penkawr-Che smiled. "But I don't trust *you* either, and I think if I sent my men away you'd be gone in an instant, without finishing the map. So I'll tell you what we'll do. In exactly one minute, I shall send men after Ashton; the stunners will put you down, here and now, and we'll begin this whole weary business over again." He pointed to a small array of weapons that had been placed on the ground at a safe distance. "You won't live long without those. Finish the map, pick them up, and walk away free."

Stark's fingers closed on the stylus until it seemed that it must snap. His head dropped forward and his eyes narrowed.

Penkawr-Che said, "It's Ashton who will suffer. Shall I give the order?"

Stark let out a harsh breath and bent over the map.

Penkawr-Che smiled again, briefly. Imperceptibly, the men relaxed. They knew now what they were going to do.

"All right, damn you," Stark said, in a low and furious voice. "Look." Penkawr-Che looked, where

Stark was pointing with the stylus. "The Citadel is a burned-out ruin, but you can find it behind the mists of the Thermal Pits. From the Citadel, so . . ."

The stylus began a straight, sure line.

Stark's left hand struck the heavy lamp and knocked it straight into Penkawr-Che's startled grasp. The golden man cried out with pain and dropped it from his seared hands.

Stark was already moving, so swiftly that the eye could scarcely follow him. Instead of going for the weapons, he flung himself directly at the man who stood nearest him. The man, watching Stark, had perforce been staring into the light, which was now on the ground, still shining though partly hidden by the case. During the split second in which his vision was attempting to deal with the sudden change, Stark slammed into him low across the body. The man went over, loosing off his stunner at the sky. Stark rushed off, a large animal running low in erratic leaps and swerves, into the coarse grass with the flower-eyes.

An ordinary man, even a skillful one, could hardly have found cover there. But this was N'Chaka, who had found cover on naked rock when the four-pawed death came snuffling after him. Like the four-pawed death, he moved as he had done so many times before when he played at the game of survival, aping the pursuer-quarry, sliding flat and hugging the ground.

The glare behind him wavered and flashed as the lamp was set up again, worse for the marksmen than no light at all. They were firing wild, in any case, having lost sight of him almost at once; they had placed too much confidence in their numbers and in the futility of any attempt to escape, basing their estimate on human reflexes as they knew them. Stark had gambled his reflexes against theirs, and for the moment he had won. He was quickly out of range of the stunners.

The long-range weapons now began to crack. Dirt spurted up in little fountains, some so close that he was pelted, others so distant that he knew the men were aiming systematically to cover a given area rather than to hit a specific target. Some of the fire went into the clump of thorn where Ashton had last been seen, but Stark knew that Ashton would not be there now.

In the shelter of a hollow, he stripped off the pale-colored tunic, rolled it small and stuck it in his belt. The light had steadied behind him. High up, the illumination was clear. At ground level, it was streaked and patched with the shadows thrown by each small inequality in the surface, so that the marksmen were firing into a distracting pattern of dark and bright. Stark kept as much as possible to the dark.

More weapons had joined the original two. In the intervals of firing he could hear a great deal of shouting. Then this faded and became distant, like the light, though the firing still kept up. When Stark was well past the clump of thorns and into honest night, he began to make a low hissing sound that was like the voice of the four-pawed death but cadenced as a recognition signal. He continued to make it until Ashton's voice spoke to him from the lip of a small gully.

Stark slid down into it.

Ashton had removed his own tunic and rubbed his pale skin with handsful of soil. He had not forgotten the lessons of his active youth.

"That was the most beautiful sound I ever heard," he said, and put his hand briefly on Stark's shoulder. "Now what?"

"Go to ground," Stark said, and glanced at the sky. "We're about out of darkness."

They scrambled along the gully to where it opened onto more of the coarse grass and pallid, staring flowers. A thick clump of thorn stood at the mouth of the gully, but Stark kept on past it.

Ashton stopped abruptly. "Listen!"

From behind them, where the tall ship was, came the muffled throb and thump of motors waked to sudden life.

"Yes," said Stark. "The hoppers."

He ran on, as the first of the Three Ladies thrust the edge of her shining countenance gently above the horizon.

5

The Three Ladies are Skaith's crowning beauty, in fact her only one—three magnificent star-clusters that grace the moonless sky, shedding a light more sweet and silvery than Old Sun's rusty glare, but almost as bright. Darkness is hard to come by on Skaith, even at night.

It did not much matter now. Darkness would not save them from the hoppers.

They found more clumps of twisted thorn, shadowed and tempting. Stark ignored them. A low ridge rose to the right, silhouetted against the distant glow around *Arkeshti*. Stark ignored that, too. He stayed on the open, exposed slope. Not much of a slope, but enough to have carried off superficial drainage in the rainy season.

The throb of the motors changed. The hoppers were airborne.

"Here," Stark said, thrusting Ashton down into a barely perceptible wrinkle in the ground.

He tore up clods of grass and flowers and strewed them over Ashton, enough to break up the visual aspect of a human body. He spoke a single word to Ashton, a click-cough sound that meant *freeze*. Then he slid away up to the ridge.

From there he observed a great deal of activity around the ship. Men with lights were already on the heath, beating back and forth; and others were coming to join them, searching for dead or wounded bodies.

Up above them, the four hoppers had switched on

their powerful landing beams. They swept out into a long line, rushing ahead of the men. Their loud-hailers boomed and belled, an unnatural baying like the voices of some strange breed of mechanized hound hot on the scent. Bolts from their laser cannon struck downward and clumps of thorn erupted into dust and flame.

Stark left the ridge in haste. He found another shallow fold in the slope, not enough to conceal a rabbit, but he dug himself in with his fingers as best he could and lay still among the grass and flowers.

The roar of the hoppers filled the sky, sweeping back and forth, pounding the coverts flat. One of the hoppers paused over the gully, shining down its white glare, pulverizing the shadows with flaring lightning bolts. The loud-hailer shouted Stark's name, then laughed. Stark thought the voice was Penkawr-Che's, but the metallic distortion was such that he could not be sure. The thorn thickets which had seemed to offer such tempting concealment went up, one after the other, in a rage of flame.

The fires and the edges of the landing beams lit up the slope clearly enough even without the Lady's cluster light. Stark lay and listened to the pounding of his own heart, and prayed that Ashton could lie as still as he, and as long; the hunters would be alert for movement. Habitually, Stark knew from the experience of a lifetime, they looked for two things: cover where the quarry may be hiding, or the quarry itself, caught in the open, running. They seldom looked too closely where there is neither cover nor movement, no place to hide, nothing to see. That was why Stark had chosen to remain in the open.

But the price of invisibility is complete lack of motion. Once the quarry stirs, it is lost.

A pair of yellow birds forgot that axiom. Panicked by the noise and flames, they broke and rushed diagonally upward across the slope. The loud-hailer hallooed, and a laser bolt—in massive overkill—crisped them to cinders.

The hopper hung, swinging about, questing. Apparently Ashton did not stir, for nothing else caught its attention and it roared on to devour fresh ground.

Stark continued to lie without moving. Loose dirt trickled from the clods with which he had camouflaged himself. Small disturbed things crawled on him. Some of them bit. The dark-eyed flowers peered this way and that in wild disarray; perhaps the air currents generated by the hopper were responsible. There was a smell of smoke in the air. Fire was spreading out from the thorn thickets, and the shot that killed the birds had set the grass alight. Stark could hear the crackling, entirely too close for comfort. He tried to assess the degree of dryness of the grass, hoping the flames would not spread too quickly. The line of search was drawing away, but the hoppers were bound to come back. It was too soon to move.

The flowers looked down at him from around his face. They looked over him at the fires. They looked upward at the sky. Certainly flowers did not see, but they might have other sensors. They also had a faint sticky fragrance that became more insistent as Stark breathed it, even under the taint of smoke. He also had the unpleasant sensation that the grass crept against him like a sentient thing, touching him with its blades. He had a very great desire to be on his feet again, and away from this too-great intimacy.

Smoke began to blow across him. He forgot his other discomforts in the effort not to cough, and he believed the crackling sound was louder. Little puffs of heat touched his skin.

The hoppers, having gone well past the point where their quarry might have run, wheeled round. They went more slowly on the way back, rummaging leisurely about the ruined landscape, making sure they had left no cover where a man might live. One of them came across the slope and speared Stark in the direct glare of the landing beam.

He held his breath, and shut his eyes, lest they catch the light and shine. Smoke rolled across him—

and that was good in one way—but he could feel
the heat of the ground now with his feet. In a few
moments the flames would be all around him. The
grass and the flowers knew it, too; he had no further
doubt that they were in some manner aware and
cringing. He grappled with the panic that rose within
him and held it down; then, after a lazy eternity, the
hopper droned on over the ridge, back toward
Arkeshti.

Even so, Stark did not move until he could smell
the soles of his boots smoldering. Then he had no
further choice. Still in the thick smoke, he bolted out
of his shallow grave and hurried along to where he
had left Ashton, knowing that if another hopper
chanced by they would have no hope.

The fire had not yet spread near to Ashton, who
had not moved. He rose up stiffly when Stark bent
over him, and was obliged to stamp about in order
to loosen his muscles.

"When I used to go hunting with the abos," he said
wryly, "I was somewhat younger. Otherwise, Four-
Paws would have eaten me." He shivered. "That last
one was too close for comfort! Thank God for the
smoke."

They set off, away from the ship, threading their
way between fires and over patches of scorched
ground. They heard no further sound of motors in
the sky. Having stamped the land flat, the hunters
could assume that the quarry had perished in one or
another of the flaming coverts.

Presently Stark and Ashton were beyond the
perimeter of the fires. They kept on until it became
apparent that Ashton, who had not had an easy day,
was beginning to flag. Stark found a thicket, made
sure that nothing laired in it, and sat down so the
thorn-trees guarded his back. Penkawr-Che's poisons
were still in his blood, so he was glad of the rest.

The flowers had marked their passage. Long ripples
ran across them, streaming far away, out of sight; but

there was nothing strange in this except that the ripples ran crosswise to the wind.

Ashton said, "Eric, when I was lying there pretending not to exist, with the grass and flowers close against me, I got the feeling that—"

"So did I. There's some kind of sentience there. Maybe the sort of thing that tells a Venus flytrap when to snap shut."

"Do you suppose they're carrying a message? And if so, to whom?"

The heath stretched away on all sides, tilting toward the horizon, rough and rumpled, dotted with the twisted thickets and occasional blasted trees. Stark lifted his head and quartered the wind, scenting strangeness, scenting nothing welcoming to man. The faint and somehow treacherous sweetness of the flowers —endless miles of them—caught in his throat. There was nothing in all that emptiness to catch the eye, and yet he sensed presences, things awake and knowing. Whether these were human, animal, or quite other, he could not tell.

He did not like it. "I'll be glad to leave this upland," he said, "and by the quickest way."

"That's the way we just came," said Ashton. "Penkawr-Che picked his spot because the hoppers can raid down into the jungle on about a 180-degree perimeter without having to go much more than a hundred miles in any direction. Eventually, the other two ships, which are raiding elsewhere, will rendezvous with him and they'll head north together to see if they can crack that treasure-house under the Witchfires. How much did you have to tell him?"

"Not as much as he wanted. With luck, he might find that balcony within half a year." Stark frowned. "I don't know . . . The Diviners said that I would bring more blood to the House of the Mother. That's why they tried so hard to kill me. Well, they must fight their battles. We've got one of our own to worry about." He swept his hand across the limitless horizon.

"We can't go eastward because of Penkawr-Che. Otherwise, we have a free choice. Any suggestions?"

"Pedrallon."

"What about Pedrallon?"

"He's a prince in his own country. His people bought him back from Penkawr-Che. He has position and power—"

"Unless his people decided to feed him to Old Sun for his sins."

"I suppose it's possible, but he's the only person I can think of who might help us, and who is also located where we might conceivably reach him. Andapell lies along the coast somewhere southwest of here."

"How far?"

"I don't know. But we could strike for the coast and perhaps get passage on a ship. Or, failing that, steal a boat."

"The last time I saw Pedrallon," said Stark, "he had very little use for off-worlders even though he was intriguing with them for his own ends. He will have even less use for them now."

"I came to know him quite well, Eric. There was a lot of time aboard ship, while Penkawr-Che was making up his mind whether to take us to Pax and be satisfied with the payment he'd been promised, or to gamble on his heaven-sent opportunity to loot a world. I think I gave Pedrallon a better understanding of what the Galactic Union is and how it works, and I think he came rather to like me as an individual. Also, he is a dedicated man, to the point of fanaticism. He swore he would go on fighting the Wandsmen, even though his hopes of ever achieving the freedom of starflight are gone. He might even find us useful."

"A faint hope, Simon."

"Worse than faint. But do we have another?"

Stark brooded. "Irnan has nothing left to fight with. Tregad and the other city-states are an unknown quantity. They may go either way. In any case, as you say, they're out of reach." He shrugged. "It might as well be Andapell."

Stark let Ashton sleep for an hour. During that time he rattled around the thicket and, by dint of tearing his hands painfully, managed to fashion two clubs from thorn-wood, snapped to the proper length beneath his boot heel. When he could find the right kind of shattered stone, he would be able to provide hand axes or knife-blades as well. In the meantime, the clubs were a comfort.

The heath was without landmarks, a country in which a man might easily lose himself and wander until he died, unless something took him first, and unaware. Here in the outer reaches of the galaxy the starfields were thin, but Stark found enough old friends to set a course by. When he roused Ashton, they headed west and south, away from *Arkeshti,* hoping to reach the rim of the upland, where it dropped down to the jungle that lay between it and the sea. Neither one had any idea how far that rim might be.

But Stark remembered how, months before, he and Ashton had set out together from the Citadel, far in the bitter north, two men alone on a hostile planet. Then, they had had weapons and supplies, and beasts of burden—and they had had the Northhounds. Now they were destitute, and all the labors of that earlier journey had been brought to nothing by the treachery of one man.

Stark's bitterness was not alleviated by the knowledge that he himself had made the arrangements with Penkawr-Che.

With all the persuasion of his considerable wealth, the Wandsman Pedrallon had not been able to talk the Antarean into getting involved in Skaith's problems beyond providing a transceiver and keeping a speculative finger on the pulse of things. Only Stark's last-minute intervention, when the starport was already in flames and the ships in the act of departure, had tipped the scales, along with his mention of Ashton's rescue and the rewards to be won by Penkawr-Che through taking him and the delegations to Galactic Center. Stark could not have known what sort of man Penkawr-Che was, and in any case the Antarean had been the only hope available. But these thoughts made Stark no happier now.

He glanced sidelong at his foster-father, who ought by now to have been almost within sight of Pax and his office at the Ministry of Planetary Affairs.

"It comes to my mind, Simon," he said, "that if all I saved you for was to walk Skaith perpetually like some landbound Flying Dutchman, I might better have left you with the Lords Protector, where at least your captivity was comfortable."

"As long as my legs hold out," said Ashton, "I'd rather walk."

The flowers watched them, rippling. The last of the Three Ladies rose, adding her silvery light to that of her sisters. The heath was flooded with gentle radiance.

Nevertheless, the night seemed very dark.

6

The gray old city of Irnan crouched above the valley. The circle of her walls was unbroken, but the landing of *Arkeshti* had accomplished in a matter of hours what months of siege and suffering had failed to do. Faced with the choice of renewed fighting or surrender to the forces of the Wandsmen, which would surely come, she found that in fact she had no choice. She was exhausted, stripped, denuded. She had lost too heavily of men and wealth. Above all, she had lost hope.

Under the light of the Three Ladies, a thin stream of refugees trickled steadily from the open gate and along the road that ran between ruined orchards and obliterated fields still littered with the rubbish of the besieging armies. Most of the refugees were on foot, carrying what possessions they could on their backs. They were those who felt themselves too closely associated with the revolt against the Wandsmen to hope for mercy, or who feared a general butchery when the hordes of the Farers were loosed upon them.

Within the gate, in the main square of the ctiy, where the buildings of weathered stone stood close around and a few torches burned, a company of men and women were clotted loosely together. More joined them from time to time, straggling from the dark mouths of narrow streets. These bore arms, all of them, for the women of the city-states were trained to battle like the men since they faced the same hazards from the roving Wild Bands and raiders down from the Barrens. They huddled in their cloaks in the cool night, for the valley was high and it was autumn, and they talked in low, harsh voices. Some of them wept, and not the women alone.

In the Council Hall, beneath the high vault hung with ancient banners, a scant few lamps burned, husbanding precious oil. But there was tumult enough if there was a lack of light. The floor was packed with a shouting, shoving multitude, and on the dais, where the elders sat, angry men and women crowded about, with raised voices and emphatic hands. The meeting, if it could be called that, had been going on since shortly after *Arkeshti*'s departure.

The subject was surrender. The mood was fear, the language cruel, and old Jerann was finding there his penultimate martyrdom.

Beyond the walls, the encampments of the allies were in the final stages of dismantling. Tribesmen in wrapped veils and leather cloaks dyed in the dusty colors of the Six Lesser Hearths of Kheb—purple Hann, brown Marag, yellow Qard, red Kref, green Thorn, and white Thuran—moved among guttering torches, loading their tall desert beasts with provisions and plunder.

Farther away from the city, arrogantly isolated, the dark-furred Fallarin sat muttering among themselves, striking little angry puffs of wind from out their wings. The Tarf, their agile servants in stripes of green and gold, with four powerful ropey arms apiece, did the work of breaking camp.

By morning, they would all be gone.

Beyond them all, the valley lay empty and quiet. But at its upper end, where the mountains closed in and rocky walls narrowed steeply together, was the grotto from which generations of Gerriths, wise women of Irnan, had watched over the welfare of their city.

The grotto had been robbed of all its furnishings, so that it was more than ever like a tomb. Gerrith, the last of her name, had renounced her status as wise woman, saying that her tradition had ended with the destruction of the Robe and Crown at the hands of the Wandsman Mordach. Yet there were beasts tethered below the entrance, and a dim reflection of light shone from it. On the ledge by this entrance a Tarf stood sentinel, leaning on his four-handed sword and blinking horny eyelids with the timeless patience of his kind. His name was Klatlekt.

In the outer chamber of the grotto, the anteroom, eleven great white hounds couched themselves, with drooping heads and half-lidded eyes that glowed with strange fires where they caught the light of a single lamp that burned on a high shelf. From time to time they growled and stirred uneasily. They were telepaths born and bred, and the human minds they touched were far from tranquil.

Three candles lighted the naked inner chamber, throwing wild shadows on the walls of what had once been the wise woman's sanctum. Some few items of furniture had been brought in—a table, a chair, the candelabrum, and a broad, flat basin filled with shining water. Gerrith sat in the chair, a sun-colored woman with the candle flames shining on the thick bronze braid of hair that hung down her back. She had been in this place ever since Eric John Stark walked out from the gates of Irnan into Penkawr-Che's ship. Weariness had drawn shadows at her eyes and etched tight lines about her mouth.

"I have made my decision," she said. "I await yours."

"It is not an easy choice," said Sabak, the young leader of the hooded tribesmen. Only his eyes showed between hood and veil—blue, fierce, and disturbed. His father was Keeper of the Hearth of Hann, and a power in the north. "The Wandsmen will surely try to retake Yurunna and drive us back into the desert to starve. We followed Stark, and gladly, but now it seems that we must go home and fight for our own people."

"For me," said Tuchvar, "there is no choice." He looked at the two huge hounds shouldering against him, and smiled. He was young, a boy only, and he had been an apprentice Wandsman in service to the Houndmaster of Yurunna. "The Northhounds will find N'Chaka if he lives, and I go with them."

Gerd, at his right side, made a thunderous noise in his throat. Grith, at his left, opened her muzzle wide and let her tongue hang red across her sharp teeth. Both beasts turned their lambent gaze on Halk, who stood at one end of the table.

"Keep your hellhounds leashed," he said, and turned to Gerrith. "Your mother, in this room, foretold the coming of a Dark Man from the stars, who would overthrow the Lords Protector and free Irnan, so that we might find a better world to live on. So much for your mother's prophecy, so much for the Dark Man. *I* am not in love with Stark, to waste what life I have in searching for him. My people are waiting for me. We intend to go on fighting the Wandsmen, at Tregad or wherever else we can. I would advise you to come with us, or to go north with Sabak and the Fallarin. Alderyk might even give you sanctuary at the Place of Winds."

Alderyk, King of the Fallarin, whose shadow lay upon the wall like the shadow of a great bird with brooding wings half stretched, looked at Gerrith with his falcon eyes and said, "You would be safer in the north. If you go southward, you challenge the full power of the Wandsmen."

"And what of you, Alderyk?" asked Gerrith. "Which way will you go?"

He cocked his narrow head. He had a smile like a dagger. "I have not yet heard the prophecy. For there is a prophecy, is there not? You would not have called us all here to speak of Stark unless there were one."

"Yes," said Gerrith. "There is a prophecy." She rose up, standing tall in the candlelight, and the hounds whimpered. "I have seen my own path in the Water of Vision. It lies south, and then south, into a terrible whiteness stained with blood, and the end of it is hidden in the mist. But I have looked beyond the Water of Vision."

Between her two hands she held a skull, a small frail thing carved in yellowed ivory and worn with the passing of much time. Its tiny, grinning face was flecked with old blood.

"This is the last fragment of the Crown of Fate. Stark brought it to me from the gallows, on the day we slew our Wandsmen. All the Gerriths who once wore that crown now speak to me through it. Their power has come to me at last." Her voice rang, clear and strong, with a haunting melancholy, a bell heard across hills when the wind is blowing.

"Halk has said that the Prophecy of Irnan was false, and that Stark is a failed and useless man, to be discarded and forgotten. I tell you that this is not so. I tell you that Stark's fate and the fate of Irnan are bound together as heart and breath are bound, and one shall not survive without the other. Stark lives, and *his* way, too, lies southward. But he walks in a great darkness, and death lies ahead of him. His salvation depends on us. If he lives to walk that southern road, Irnan will yet be free. If he dies"—she made a gesture of finality—"the star-roads will not be open in our time, nor in any time until long after the face of Skaith has changed—and that change is coming. The Goddess moves, my lady Cold with her lord Darkness and their daughter Hunger. She has sent her spies before. This winter we shall see the first of her armies. And if the starships do not come soon, there will be no escape for any of us from the Second Wandering!"

She lowered her hands and bent her head and caught a long, unsteady breath. When she looked at them again, and spoke again, she was Gerrith the woman, human and vulnerable.

"There is great need for haste," she said. "Stark moves slowly, as a man on foot, a man with a burden, amid obstacles. Yet he is far away, and even a mounted force will have difficulty reaching the sea in time—"

"The sea?" asked Halk.

"That is where our paths converge, and where his will end if we do not meet."

She moved around the table and put her hand on Gerd's massive head.

"Come," she said to Tuchvar. "We, at least, know what we must do."

They went into the anteroom, Gerd and Grith and Tuchvar and Gerrith; the other eleven Northhounds rose and joined them. They walked out onto the ledge, into the light of the Three Ladies, past the impassive Klatlekt, and down toward the tethered riding animals.

A buffet of wind plucked at Gerrith's garments and rumpled the coarse fur of the hounds. They looked up.

"I will consult with my people," said Alderyk. He came flapping down the path with Klatlekt behind him.

Halk followed, cursing. Sabak, silent, followed him.

"In one hour," said Gerrith, "we start south, Tuchvar and the hounds and I. We will not wait."

They rode away, severally, along the valley. The dim light continued to shine from the entrance to the grotto. No one had thought to blow out the candles or extinguish the lamp, or cover over the Water of Vision. And not even the wise woman gave a backward glance.

The last prophecy of Irnan had been made.

7

Stark awoke instantly at the touch of Ashton's hand.

The grudging rebirth of Old Sun stained the heath with a level flood of bloody light. The birds stood in it, their plumage touched to a burning gold on one side, shadows flung darkly on the other. There were about thirty of them. They watched the two men from a distance of a hundred feet or so, the flowers nodding around them.

"They came so quietly," said Ashton, who had been on watch. "I didn't realize they were there until the sun came up."

There was something unnatural about the silence of the birds, and their patience. Stark would have expected them to be noisy with greed and excitement. He would have expected them to attack. Instead, they simply stood there, unreal in that unreal light that caused the landscape to appear tilted and foreshortened, depthless, like a tapestry with golden birds embroidered on it.

Stark took up his club. He searched for stones.

One of the birds lifted its head and sang, in a very clear and flutelike voice—the voice of a woman singing through a bird's throat. The song had no words. Yet Stark straightened, frowning.

"I think we've been forbidden to kill," he said, and clicked two stones together in his hand, measuring the distance.

"I felt the same thing," Ashton said. "Perhaps we ought to listen?"

46

Stark was hungry. The yellow birds represented both food and menace. He did not know what they would do if he did kill one of them, for they were numerous and powerful. If he provoked an attack, it would not be easy to fight them off. Besides, they seemed to have some purpose, and that wordless song had struck a note of strangeness which made him reluctant to do anything rash until he knew more about what was afoot.

He said irritably, "For a while, at least." And he dropped the stones.

"They're in our way," said Ashton.

The birds had ranged themselves to the southwest.

"Perhaps they'll scatter," Stark suggested.

He started walking. So did Ashton.

The birds did not scatter. They stood high on their strong legs and opened their curved beaks, clashing them together with a harsh and threatening sound.

Stark halted, and the birds were still.

"We can fight them," he said, "or we can go another way."

Ashton put his hand on his tunic, over the bandages. He said, "Their claws are very sharp, and I see thirty double sets of them. Their beaks are like knives. Let's try another way."

"Perhaps we can circle them."

They tried that. The flock raced to turn them back.

Ashton shook his head. "When the bird attacked me, it was acting according to its normal instincts. These are not acting in any normal way at all."

Stark looked about him at the heath, the twisted thorn and the skeletal trees, the peering flowers that blew as they listed with no regard for the wind.

"Someone knows we're here," he said. "Someone has sent for us."

Ashton weighed his club and sighed. "I don't think I could knock down enough of those brutes, and I'd like to keep my eyes yet a while. Perhaps the *someone* only wants to talk to us?"

"If that's so," said Stark, "it will be the first time since I came to Skaith."

The bird lifted up its head and sang again.

Perhaps, Stark thought, it was the natural voice of the creature. But the feeling that some greater intelligence was speaking through it was inescapable. *Do as I ask*, it seemed to say, *and no harm shall come to you*. Stark trusted it not at all. Alone, he might have chosen to gamble on fighting his way through, even though the odds were formidable. As it was, he shrugged and said, "Well, perhaps we'll get fed, anyway."

The birds, thirty careful herd-dogs, drove them on, westerly across the heath. They moved at a good pace. Stark kept one eye and ear cocked at the sky in case Penkawr-Che decided to send the hoppers for a final look around. None appeared. Apparently Penkawr-Che felt that plundering villagers of their valuable drug crop was more to the point than searching for two men who were almost certainly dead, and who, if they were not now, soon would be. In any case, the chance of their being rescued and flown back to Pax was so remote that while Penkawr-Che would have killed them out-of-hand when he had them, it was not likely that he would mount any full-scale search for them. If nothing else, he lacked the time and manpower.

Old Sun sat glaring in the middle of the sky and Simon Ashton was beginning to stumble in his walk, when Stark saw two figures silhouetted on the crest of a rise before them. One was tall, with long hair and flowing robes that blew in the wind. The other was smaller and slighter, and the taller one stood protectively with one hand on its shoulder. They stood quite alone, with something regal in their aloneness and their proud bearing.

The birds made little glad sounds and drove the men onward more quickly.

The tall figure became a woman, neither beautiful nor young. Her face was lean and brown, with an

immense strength, the strength of wood seasoned to
an iron toughness. The wind pressed coarse brown
garments against a body that was like a tree trunk,
with meager breasts and thin hips and a powerful
straightness as though it had fronted many gales and
withstood them. Her eyes were brown and piercing,
and her hair was brown with streaks of frost.

The slighter figure was a boy of perhaps eleven
years, and he was sheer beauty, bright and fresh and
graceful, but with a curious calmness in his gaze that
made his eyes seem far too old for his child's face.

Stark and Ashton halted below these two, so that
they were looking up and the woman and the boy
were looking down, a nice positioning psychologically,
and the bird sang once more.

The woman answered, in the sweet identical tone,
without words. Then she studied the men, with a
sword-thrust glance, and said, "You are not sons of
Mother Skaith."

Stark said, "No."

She nodded. "This was the strangeness my messengers sensed." She spoke to the boy, and in her manner
were both love and deference. "What is your thought,
my Cethlin?"

He smiled gently and said, "They are not for us,
Mother. Another has set her seal upon them."

"Well, then," said the woman, turning again to Stark
and Ashton, "be welcome, for a time." She beckoned
to them with the stateliness of a bending tree. "I am
Norverann. This is my son Cethlin, my last and
youngest, who is called the Bridegroom."

"The Bridegroom?"

"Here we worship the Trinity—my lady Cold and
her lord Darkness, and their daughter Hunger, who
come to rule us. My son will go to the Daughter in
his eighteenth year, if she does not claim him sooner."

"She will, Mother," said the calm-eyed boy. "The
day is close at hand."

He moved away from her, disappearing below the

crest. Norverann waited. Stark and Ashton climbed
to where she stood.

They looked down into a long hollow set with
tents and pavilions. Beyond the hollow, clearly visible,
was the edge of the plateau, which had curved round
to meet them, so that they had not actually come far
out of their way. Beyond the rough and channeled
edge was a soaring emptiness of air, and beneath that,
distant and misty, a greenness reflecting from a sea of
treetops.

The encampment itself formed a rough semi-circle
round an open space, where men and women busied
themselves and children played. The colors of the
pavilions were brown and green and russet, with here
and there a gleam of gold or white, or a touch of
scarlet, and menders had been at work sewing new
seams and setting patches. But each tent was adorned
with garlands and sheaves of grain. Baskets of roots
and other things were set before them. Tattered
pennons fluttered in the wind.

"A festival?" asked Stark.

"We celebrate," said Norverann, "the Death of
Summer."

Between the points of the semi-circle, beyond the
open space and close to the edge of the plateau, was
a structure of cut stone. It crouched close to the
ground, somehow ominous in its squat windowless
strength, covered like an ancient boulder with moss
and lichens.

"That is the House of Winter," said Norverann.
"It is almost time for us to return to the blessed
darkness and the sweet sleep." She bent in her stately
fashion to touch the nodding flowers, which swayed
toward her. "We share the sacred months of the
Goddess with the grasses and the birds and all things
dwelling on the heath."

"They are your messengers?"

She nodded. "Long ago we learned the lesson of our
kinship. On the heath we are all one, parts of the
same body, the same life. When violence was done to

the eastern extremity of our body, the message was brought to us here. Burning and destruction, the slaughter of many grasses and flowers and families of thorn. You will tell me about that." She turned her gaze toward Stark and Ashton, and it was as cold and cruel as the sharpest edge of winter. "If you were not already claimed, there would be punishment."

"It was not our doing," Stark said. "Other men were hunting us. We barely escaped with our lives. But who has claimed us, and for what?"

"You must ask Cethlin." She led them down from the ridge to a pavilion of mossy green, and she lifted aside a curtain of dull umber. "Please to enter, and make yourselves fit for the day. Water will be brought to you for washing—"

"Lady," said Stark, "we are hungry."

"You will be fed," she told him, "in good time." She dropped the curtain and was gone.

The pavilion was furnished with no more than a few rough pallets stuffed with something dry and crackly, and a store of blankets. There was dust about, but it was clean dust and the air smelled of the same things it had smelled of outside. Small personal articles were arranged neatly by the pallets. The pavilion was apparently a summer dormitory for upward of a score of persons.

Ashton threw himself down on somebody's bed with a sigh of relief.

"The promise of food is at least hopeful. And since it seems we're promised to somebody else, I gather our lives are safe for the moment. So far, so good." He added, with a twist of his mouth, "Still and all, I don't like this place."

"Neither," said Stark, "do I."

Men came presently with ewers and basins and towels. The towels were of coarse cloth, as were the shapeless tunics and leg-wrappings of the men. The ewers and basins were of gold, beautifully shaped and chased with graceful designs worn almost invisible by the handling of centuries. The golden things glowed beautifully in the mossy gloom of the pavilion.

"We are called Nithi, the People of the Heath," said one of the men, in answer to Ashton's question.

The man, like Norverann, had the look of old wood, knotty and enduring, and there was something about his eyes, brown and secret, and his mouth, which was broad-lipped and square, with strong spade teeth, that gave an impression of kinship with unknown elemental things—soil and roots and hidden water, and the dark spaces below.

"Do you have trade with the jungle folk?" Stark asked, and the man smiled slowly.

"Trade," he said, "from which they get little gain."

"Do you eat them?" Stark asked matter-of-factly, and the man shrugged.

"They worship Old Sun. We rededicate them, to the Goddess."

"You must have a way down to the jungle, then."

"That is so," said the man. "Sleep now."

He went away with the others, taking the golden vessels. The sides of the pavilion flapped in the wind. The voices of the folk outside seemed faraway and unfamiliar.

Ashton shook his head. "Old Mother Skaith is still full of surprises, and few of them pleasant. That boy, the Bridegroom, who goes to the Daughter in his eighteenth year—unless she claims him sooner—sounds like ritual sacrifice."

"The boy seems to be looking forward to it," said Stark. "You'd better sleep, if you're not too hungry."

Ashton pulled a ragged blanket over him and lay quiet.

Stark watched the slack cloth of the roof billow under the wind, and he thought about Gerrith. He hoped she was well away from Irnan. He hoped she would be safe.

He thought about a lot of things, and felt the anger rising in him so strongly that it became a fever and a throbbing, and the mossy gloom turned reddish in his eyes. Because the anger was useless, he forced it away. Because sleep was necessary, he slept.

He woke with a snarl and a lunge; and there was a man's neck between his hands, ready for the breaking.

8

Ashton's voice said quietly, "Eric, he's unarmed."

The man's face stared at Stark, already darkening, its mouth and eyes stretched with the beginnings of fear. His body was rigid, trying to accommodate the throttling grip it had not yet considered resisting. The Nithi had a reaction time more suited to trees than to fighting animals.

Stark grunted and let go. "You were crouching over me," he said.

The man sucked air and hugged his throat. "I was curious," he whispered, "to see a man from another world. Besides, you are on my bed" He looked at Ashton. "Is he, too, from another world?"

"Yes."

"But you are not alike."

"Are all men of Skaith alike?"

He thought about that, rubbing his throat.

Stark was aware now of the sound of music from outside, sweet and melancholy, and a murmur of voices gathered and purposeful rather than scattered at random. There was also a smell of cooking.

"No," said the man, "of course they're not, but that has nothing to do with foreigners." He was young and supple, with the secret brown eyes Stark was beginning to dislike intensely. "I am Ceidrin, brother to the Bridegroom. I am to bring you to the feast."

He led the way out of the pavilion, his shoulders stiff. He did not look back to see whether he was followed.

Old Sun was going down in his customary senile fury of molten brass and varying shades of copper and red. Some two hundred men and women, and half as many children, were gathered in the open space between the pavilions and the glooming House of Winter. They faced Old Sun. Atop a pillar of eroded rock a fire burned. Cethlin stood beside it. Behind him stood Norverann, holding one of the golden ewers. The music had ceased. After a moment of intense silence it began again, small flat drums and pipes and two instruments with many strings; and this time it was neither sweet nor melancholy. It was strident, hard, clashing

It sank into the background, and the people began to chant.

"Old Sun goes down in darkness, may he never return. Old Sun dies, may he never live again. May the hand of the Goddess strike him, may the breath of the Goddess shrivel him. May the peace of the Goddess be upon Skaith, may it be upon us all . . ."

Cethlin took the golden ewer from his mother's hands.

At the exact moment when the disk of the ginger star vanished below the horizon, he drowned the fire on the pillar top.

"Old Sun is dead," the people chanted. *"He will not rise again. The Goddess will give us peace this night. There will not be a morning . . ."*

Water and steaming ash ran down the sides of the pillar.

When the chanting was finished, Stark asked Ceidrin, "Do you do this every night?"

"Every night aboveground."

"Most people pray Old Sun up in the morning, glad of another day."

"The Goddess will punish them."

Stark shivered. He had felt the breath of the Goddess, what time Hargoth the Corn-King and his sorcerer-priests had sent it upon the wagons of Amnir, the trader out of Komrey, and Amnir with all his

men and beasts had been received into the peace of
the Goddess with the cold rime glittering on their
faces. But even Hargoth had sacrificed to Old Sun,
lest the Dark Trinity conquer the land too soon. The
Nithi, apparently, were possessed of a full-blown death
wish.

The people were finding places on the ground now,
around large squares of heavy cloth spread there.
Yellow birds wandered among them unconcernedly.
Cauldrons steamed over thorn-wood fires.

Ashton sniffed. "I wonder what's in those pots."

"Whatever it is," Stark warned, "eat it."

Ceidrin motioned them to sit between Cethlin and
Norverann. The food was served in vessels of stone
which were ground fine and thin, and in baskets of
woven reeds which must have been brought up from
the jungles below. Coarse unleavened bread was served,
with bits of Mother Skaith still in it to grate the
teeth, as well as a stew made of grain and vegetables
and a minute amount of meat, which was white and
stringy and came on small brittle bones. Stark glanced
from the portion he held to the companionable birds.

"We ask their pardon," said Norverann, "as we
ask pardon of the grain when we reap it, and the
growing things when we tear them from the ground.
They understand. They know that they will feed on us
one day." She made a circling motion with her hand.
"We are all the same, each in his season."

"And your son," asked Ashton. "When his time
comes, will you strike the knife into his heart yourself?"

"Of course," said Norverann, and Cethlin looked at
him in mild-eyed amazement.

"Who else," he asked, "should have that honor?"

Stark ate, and the yellow birds pecked around him,
eyeing him sidelong, aware of his alienage. The
musicians finished their meal and picked up their
instruments again. A woman rose and began to sing,
her voice carrying like a flute above the gabble of
voices.

"Now," said Norverann, "I wish to know what forces threaten our eastern body."

Stark explained to her as well as he could. "I think they will do no more damage, except for the landing of the other two ships when they come. Soon after that, they will be gone."

"Gone from the heath. But from Skaith?"

"Yes. The Wandsmen have driven all the ships away. There will be no more."

"That is well," said Norverann. "Mother Skaith must look to her own children now."

"You have some foreknowledge?"

"Not I. But my son has heard the Goddess speaking in the night wind. She has bidden him make ready for the wedding. This winter, or the next . . . I think we have not long to wait."

Torches had been lighted. The remains of the feast were being cleared away. The music had taken on a different sound. People were rising, moving onto the open ground between the torches, arranging themselves in the pattern of a dance.

Norverann rose and spoke graciously. "You are fed? You are rested? Good. Then it is time for you to go."

Stark said, "Lady, it would be better if we could wait until the morning."

"You will have a guide," she answered, "and the Three Ladies will light your way. Ceidrin . . ."

The young man said sulkily, "I shall miss the dancing."

"The one who waits for these two must not be kept waiting. Nor must she be cheated, Ceidrin, remember that."

Stark caught the young Bridegroom by the shoulder as he moved away toward the dancers.

"Cethlin," he said, "your mother said I must ask you. Who has claimed us, and why?"

"If I told you, you might try to evade the claimant. Is that not so?" Cethlin brushed his hand away and smiled. "Go with my brother."

Ceidrin fetched a torch and called two other men. He marched off with them toward the House of Winter. Since there was no choice, Stark and Ashton gave Norverann thanks for her hospitality and followed.

They passed by the dancing place. Cethlin had reached out and taken the hand of a girl with dazed eyes and garlands in her long hair. Langorous beguiling pipes and muttering strings lured them on. Cethlin stepped out with his partner, treading the intricate pattern of a maze dance that was both graceful and sinister. The drums beat, soft and insistent, like tiny hearts.

"How will it end?" Ashton asked Ceidrin.

"The girl with the garlands—she is Summer, you understand—the girl will be led deeper and deeper into the maze until she falls exhausted."

"Will she die?"

"Not for several nights yet," Ceidrin said. "At least I shall not miss that. It is not so easy to kill the wicked season."

"Why," asked Stark, "are you all so eager for the peace of the Goddess?"

Ceidrin gave him a glance of pure scorn. "Her rule is inevitable. We seek only to hasten the day. I hope it comes in my time. But I hope that before the Goddess takes me, I may look down from this high place and see the green jungle black and shriveled, and the worshipers of Old Sun struck dead."

"There are many of them," Stark said. "All sacrificing to Old Sun to keep him going. It will be a while before the Goddess rules all Skaith. Where exactly are you taking us?"

"Down," said Ceidrin. "To the jungle. Once there, you may go where you will."

"We need weapons."

"There are none here but kitchen knives and reaping hooks—and those we cannot part with." He added, "Even if we would."

The squat and ancient bulk of the stone house swallowed them, swallowed the sound of music and

the sight of dancers treading their mazy path. Inside
was a different sort of maze, full of traps and pitfalls
to discourage any intruder. Ceidrin, with the single
flickering torch, led the way safely past these and into
a network of burrows, poor and meager in com-
parison with the magnificent caverns of the House of
the Mother, but adequate for persons who wished
only to survive the winter—though Stark doubted
that winter on the plateau was all that severe. The
sanctuary was probably rooted more in ritual than in
necessity, though food might be a problem; the heath
would be a barren enough place even in summer.

"What do you do in these dens?" he asked. "Besides the obvious."

"The flowers and the grasses rest. So do we."

In a sort of communal chamber, with a tiny fire-
place and a roof so low that Stark must bend to
avoid the interlaced and knotted roots that held it,
Ceidrin opened one of several great stone jars that
were set apart from corn bins and cisterns. The jar
was packed to the top with dried flower heads. The
compressed and dusty fragrance that rose from them
was enough in itself to make the mind reel.

"In life they bring us comradeship, in death they
bring us dreams. The winter is dark and sweet."

Reverently he replaced the lid and they passed on.
The burrows were well stocked and clean. Nevertheless, Stark did not envy the Nithi their well-adapted
lives.

They stooped their way along a narrow passage and
finally came out abruptly into the open night, on a
tiny ledge or landing like a bird's perch high above
the jungle, which showed as a vast and spreading
darkness far below. The first of the Three Ladies,
newly risen, shed enough light so that Stark could see
the way. Ashton saw it, too, and muttered something,
a curse or a prayer or both.

Ceidrin put out his torch and laid it aside, because
he needed both hands more than he needed light. He
started down.

The cliffs were broken, pitted with erosion, gashed by falls of rotten rock. The way was sometimes a path and sometimes a stair, and sometimes no more than chipped-out foot- and handholds across a leaning face. Warm air rising from below was twisted into turbulent currents that twitched and plucked at the climbers with seemingly malicious intent. Sometimes the path was cut inside the cliff, and here the wind rushed ferociously, almost hurling them bodily upward like sparks in a flue. Certain places held ingenious arrangements of ropes and windlasses, and Stark surmised that they were used to aid in the ascent of men coming back from the lowlands laden with spoil.

The great milky cluster rose higher. Her light strengthened. In the darkness below, a glimmer showed. It spread and ran, became a silver snake winding through the black. A great river, going to the sea.

"How far?" asked Stark, shouting to be heard above the rush of wind.

Ceidrin shook his head with arrogant disdain. "We have never seen the sea."

Stark marked the direction, knowing that he would lose sight of the river later on.

The third of the Three Ladies was at her zenith and the first one had already set when they reached a hole in the rock no more than fifty feet above the treetops. Inside the hole was a landing and a narrow shaft straddled by a windlass with a mass of fiber rope wound on its drum.

"I will go first," said Ceidrin, "and open the way for you."

He lighted a torch from a ready pile and sat in the sling end of the rope. The two other Nithi men, who had spoken no word all the way, cranked him down with a creaking and a clacking of ancient pawls. The rope had been spliced in many places and did not inspire confidence. Yet it held. Ashton went down, and then Stark, fending off the smooth sides that trickled with condensation, growing green slime.

A tiny chamber was at the bottom. In the torch-light, Ceidrin moved a ponderous counterweight and a stone slab tilted open.

"Go," he said, "to whatever arms await you."

9

They had come down from Irnan, across mountains wet with autumn rain, into the foothills. They were a small company. They had traveled fast and they had avoided roads and habitations wherever that was possible, swinging wide to the west, away from Skeg. But there were watchtowers, and wandering herdsmen, and hunters. And there were places where no other way existed except that beneath the wall of a fortified town, for all to see. And as they advanced into the softer lands, the population increased.

Here were more villages and more roads, and it was the time of the seasonal migration. Long lines of traders' wagons moved southward ahead of the snows that would block the high passes. Caravans of traveling whores and parties of wandering entertainers—dancers and musicians and tumblers, jugglers and singers and dark-cloaked men who practiced magical amazements—all of them with the coin of a summer's work jingling in their pockets, were returning to their winter circuits away from the nipping frosts. Bands of Farers, too, drifted toward the fat tropics, where there was plenty of food and *tlun* for the children of the Lords Protector. The Farers did not always keep to the roads, but randomly followed tracks known only to themselves. But no group of wayfarers could remain forever unnoticed and unseen, particularly not a group containing a half-dozen winged Fallarin and twelve trotting Tarf with four-handed swords, a ten of veiled riders in colored cloaks, another ten of men and women in steel and leather, and thirteen great white hounds with evil eyes, led by a boy in a blue smock.

It was only a matter of time. And Alderyk, King of the Fallarin, was not surprised when Tuchvar, who had been scouting as usual with the hounds, came back to tell them that there were men ahead.

"How many?" asked Halk.

The company halted, with a subdued clatter of gear and a creak of leather. The beasts dropped their heads and blew, glad of the rest.

Tuchvar said, "The hounds can't count. The thought was *Many*, and close by."

Alderyk looked about him. It was an excellent place for an ambush. Far behind them was the terrain of crouching hills they had traversed that morning, lion-coated hills with autumn grass dry and golden on their flanks. From the hills the party had come into the midst of a vast field of ruins where a city had died and left its bones. Here they had followed a path like a cattle trail which showed on the weedy ground. The debris of centuries had filled the city's forgotten streets and covered some of the shattered walls; vision did not run far in any direction. Obviously someone knew the way through the tangle, but it was not the newcomers, and surely now that path could lead them only to disaster.

A spire of broken masonry lifted above the lower ruins. Alderyk said, "Perhaps from there I might see how many, and where they wait."

The spire was at least two hundred yards away, beyond his power of flight.

"Lend me Gerd," he said to Tuchvar, then motioned to one of the Tarf. "There may be pitfalls. Seek me a safe path."

The Tarf trotted ahead. Alderyk clapped his beast over the rump with the tips of his leathery wings and moved off, with Klatlekt at his left side.

Gerd ranged himself on Alderyk's right, but not happily. The Northhound was uneasy in this company. The nonhuman minds of the Tarf were immune to

houndfear and their swords were very sharp and long.
The Fallarin had other powers. Gerd felt a whip of
air flick across him, rumpling his coat the wrong
way, and he shivered.

In a few moments, the ruins had hidden the others
and they were alone. The sun was hot. Small things
squeaked and chittered. Beyond these tiny sounds there
was nothing. Even the wind was still.

Men? asked Alderyk.

Not here. There.

Watch.

Twice the leading Tarf warned them around treacherous places. The spire rose higher, its jagged outline
clear against the sky.

At length Alderyk sighed and said, "Enough." He
reined in his mount and drew his small, wiry body
erect, poised on the beast's back, while Klatlekt held
its head.

Spreading his wings, Alderyk leapt into the air.

A clipped bird, he had said of himself, *a mockery*.
The controlled mutation that was to have given its
changeling children the freedom of flight had been a
cruel failure. The strong wings were not strong enough,
the light bodies were still too heavy. Instead of soaring
like eagles, the Fallarin could only flap like barnyard
fowl going to roost.

Instead of joy it was labor. Alderyk pounded the air
fiercely, feeling, as he always did, the raging frustra-
tion of not being able to do what his whole being
yearned to do. To ease this yearning, the Fallarin had
carved the cliffs of their mountain fortress, the Place
of Winds, into a thousand fantastic shapes that mim-
icked all the currents of the high air, so that they
could at least pretend to ride the whirlwind.

Yet, even so, he always felt a moment of exhilara-
tion, watching the ground drop away beneath, savor-
ing that exquisite instant when the wings seemed to
have achieved mastery at last and when *now*, for the
first time, the sky was truly his . . .

He clung, panting, to the spire at its crumbling peak. And he could see.

The level land sloped gently to a broad savannah. Beyond the ruins, half a mile away, was a village. He could see the walls and the warm color of thatched roofs. It was harvest time but there was no one in the fields.

Alderyk saw where the men were. He took time to see, marking several things. Then he looked on either side, across the ruins. Finally he flung himself outward and fluttered down, the air booming under his wings.

He rode back to where the others waited.

Drawing his dagger, he sketched a rough map with the point in a patch of dusty ground.

"There is only this one way through the ruins. The villagers must use it to get their herds to the hill pastures. Men wait here and here, inside the ruins, in concealment. Other men wait here, in the open, by the end of the path. And I think these men are mercenaries, for I saw steel glinting."

"Mercenaries," Halk said. "Word has gone ahead of us. How many?"

"Perhaps fifteen here, and fifteen here, either side of the path. And thirty more in the open."

"We've fought worse odds, even without the hounds."

"There are more. Here, in reserve, are the village men—forty or fifty. And in addition there are Farers, a score or more, scattered about. There may be still others that I could not see, but these I am sure of."

Halk frowned. "And only this one way through. You're certain of that."

"From up there it was plain. Away from this path, we would have to abandon the animals. Whether we could get through afoot I don't know, but it would take time. And they would still be on the other side of the ruins, watching for us."

"We could return to the hills and find another way entirely," Sabak suggested.

"No," said Gerrith. Her face had become stern, the bones more prominent, the eyes almost bleak, except that they were not the color for bleakness. "There is no time. Stark has reached the river."

"What river?"

She shook her head. "I don't know. But he is moving more swiftly now, much more swiftly, to the sea. We must go straight ahead."

Tuchvar leaned in the saddle to stroke Gerd's head. "The hounds will take us through."

Gerd half closed his eyes. Memory stirred, of days long gone, of another hand, another voice. A hand and voice that he had helped to still forever in the streets of Yurunna. The guilt was with him yet. He whimpered and thrust his head against Tuchvar's knee.

Houndmaster.

Good hound, said Tuchvar, and smiled. He looked at Halk. "Let us go, then."

They knew their battle order, all but the Irnanese among them, having fought their way together all the way from the northern deserts to the Fertile Belt: hounds first, then the Fallarin, and then the tribesmen.

The Irnanese objected to being fourth in line. "We are accustomed to lead," they said, and looked to Halk.

"If you wish to stand in the way of the Northhounds when they're about their business, you are free to do so," he told them, and nodded to Tuchvar.

Teach them, Gerd.

Gerd laughed, as a hound laughs, touching the Irnanese with a cold lash of fear.

"Are you content?" asked Halk.

They said they were.

"Then lead on, Tuchvar. And no one stops now— except for death."

Thirteen white hounds fled away along the path, baying. Their deep voices sounded in the ruins, rich and beautiful.

The waiting mercenaries, thick red-bearded men from some hill town along the edges of the Barrens, took sword and spear into their calloused hands. They set lozenge-shaped shields on their strong left arms.

Out beyond the ruins, on the clear ground, the second company of men readied their bows, nocking arrows to the strings. They listened to the belling of the hounds. They did not know that sound. They were brave men, yet some knot within them loosened and they trembled.

Kill? asked Tuchvar, galloping behind the hounds.

Too far. Soon.

The Fallarin rode high and forward, their wings half spread, so that they seemed to fly above their mounts. The Tarf paced them easily, carrying their huge swords like batons. The dusty cloaks of the Hann streamed out behind their striding beasts. The Irnanese rode more heavily, with a solid sound of iron.

Kill? asked Tuchvar.

Now.

Good. Send fear.

The eyes of the running hounds burned like lamps in the light of Old Sun. And the baying ceased.

In the sudden quiet the mercenaries waited, in their ambush of ruined walls. They waited one hard-held breath, hearing how close their quarry came.

Terror took them. A thunderbolt of fear, a tearing agony that turned the bowels to water and the bones to brittle ice. Fear that drove the heart to beat itself within the rib cage like a frantic bird.

Some of the men dropped where they stood. Others hurled their spears blindly and tried to run. On either side of the path, then, great white bodies leaped among them, and those who still had breath screamed —once.

The Fallarin swept by, along the path.

The second company of mercenaries, with their ready bows, began to run toward the ruins.

A wind sprang up, a whirlwind, rushing toward them. Dust and dry grass and fallen leaves flew up from the ground and spun wildly. Through the spinning, the mercenaries saw six small dark men with leathery wings. The wings moved all together, and beneath the skirling of the wind they thought they heard a singing like the very voice of storm.

They loosed their arrows at the winged men. Wind caught the shafts and flung them all away. Wind buffeted and blinded and confused, and when it had passed, the mercenaries saw the white hounds and the great swords of the Tarf and the companies of armed men.

"Throw down your arms!" Halk shouted. "Throw them down if you wish to live!"

The village men were streaming back through their own gate, trampling each other and the Farers in their haste. The mercenaries were outnumbered, and their noses twitched to the smell of sorcery. They had heard their comrades screaming among the ruins, and they saw how the jaws of the hounds were red and how they licked the redness from their muzzles, eager for more, and they saw how the eyes of the hounds glowed like coals in the sunlight. They calculated how much they had been paid, and decided that in losing half their company they had lost enough. They threw down their arms.

Gerrith rode forward. "Which one among you can guide us to the sea?"

No one spoke. But Gerd said, *There.*

Touch.

One of the men cried out and went to his knees.

"Come here," said Halk.

The man came.

"The rest of you, get gone."

The hounds struck them for sport and they went, running. When they had gone far enough, Halk moved his company on, keeping out of bowshot of the village wall.

"You have strong magic," said the mercenary trotting by his stirrup. "But from now on you are hunted men."

"You shall tell us," said Halk, "about that hunting."

10

Stark and Ashton had reached the river when the morning mists were rising. They saw nothing but a muddy bank and a broad swirl of brown water gliding, and the sounds of a world awakening. There was not even anything with which two men lacking knives or axes might cobble together a raft.

Stark listened, and sniffed the heavy air. "We'll rest awhile."

They had rested along the way, but not enough. Ashton's face was gray.

"If something comes to eat me," he said, "don't wake me until just before the jaws close."

He lay between the buttressing roots of a huge tree and slept. Stark leaned his back against the tree and slept also, but lightly. A warm, sluggish breeze stroked his skin with uncleanness, and the taste of it in his mouth had the deceitful sweetness of poison.

Something rustled.

He was awake in an instant. Some creature moved in the undergrowth. It was neither large nor menacing, and it was perhaps thirty feet away, upwind.

Stark moved toward it, delicate as a stalking cat.

He did not know what it was, except that it was furry and fat and had a warm smell. It bustled down to the river to drink and he pounced and caught it and broke it between his hands. The flesh was not very appetizing but he ate it, saving the best bits for Ashton.

"Field rations," he said, when Ashton woke. "I'm sorry there's no fire."

He might have made one, but apart from the time it would have taken to search for the materials, it did not seem the best part of wisdom. People are apt to be curious about strange smokes.

Ashton muttered something about getting old and soft, but he choked the raw meat down as Stark buried the debris. They drank—as little as possible, for the water had a foul taste—and then they continued on downstream, sweating in the unaccustomed heat, fighting the undergrowth, and keeping an eye out for things that might be unpleasant to tread upon.

After an hour or two they came to the trail.

It was old and well-used, worn deep in the jungle floor and beaten to a glassy smoothness. It came from somewhere to the northeast to meet the river bank and follow it south. Stark and Ashton took to it, grateful for the easy going but wary nonetheless.

Several more trails came into it from the east, and it widened with each one until it became almost a road. Stark scouted ahead at each bend, distrusting what might lie beyond.

Even so, he smelled the clearing long before he saw it.

"Carrion," he said. "A lot of it. And ripe."

Ashton grunted. "It would ripen quickly in this climate."

They went along the green-shadowed tunnel under the trees, stepping softly. Stark could hear voices clashing and quarreling. The voices of scavengers. When they came to the end of the road and saw the temple and the sacred grove, the carrion-eaters were the only things that moved there.

The temple was small and exquisite, built of wood wonderfully carved and gilded, but the ceremonies depicted in those carvings that were still whole were unpleasant in the extreme. The temple had been seared with fire and its ivory doors were shattered. The bodies of priests and servants, or the rags of them, were strewn across the steps and the ground below as if they had stood there together in a posture of defense. The tongue of fire had licked them, too.

"Penkawr-Che's work."

"Off-world work, anyway. Since we're not looking for treasure, perhaps they've left something we can use."

The scavengers flapped and growled, undisturbed.

The sacred grove—many small trees grown together in a tangle, or a single tree monstrously multiplied—drooped languidly in the heat. The trunks were smooth and pale, lovely shapes of alabaster trailing graceful branches with feathery leaves.

The temple and grove appeared desolate, peaceful with the peace of death. And yet Stark did not move out of the shelter of the jungle.

"Something?"

"I don't know." He smiled briefly. "I've grown too dependent on the hounds. Stay close."

He moved out across the compound, past the sacred grove. Sunlight struck across the alabaster trunks, showing veins of a darker shade. In the shadows between them he glimpsed pale forms that were not trees, held spiderlike in a webbed embrace of branches. He saw a girl's long dark hair. But nothing within the grove stirred or spoke.

"It's true, then," he said.

"What is?"

"The tale I heard in the north, that in this country the trees eat men." He looked at the scattered human carrion by the temple, amid singed shreds of priestly robes. "I don't feel quite so much pity for them as I did."

" 'And every tree holy with human blood,' " said Ashton, and held his nose. "Let's get on with it."

They skirted the grove, keeping well out of reach of the branches. Beyond it they came into the open space before the temple, where the scavengers fed and marks were on the ground to show where a hopper had landed. The ivory doors of the temple hung open onto darkness.

The scavengers hopped and scuttered away, protesting. Then, suddenly, in the midst of that raucous screeching came another voice, wilder, higher, more demented. A man ran out of the temple door and down the steps. He came in a headlong rush, naked, smeared with ashes, streaked with his own blood where he had gashed his flesh, and he held in his hands a great, heavy sword with a butcher's blade.

"Murderers!" he screamed. "Demons!" And he raised the sword high.

Stark thrust Ashton aside. He caught up a morsel of carrion from the littered ground, a gnawed skull, and he hurled it fair in the man's face so that he had to bring his arms down to shield himself. He broke stride and Stark ran at him. The man slashed out with the blade. Stark twisted in mid-leap and came in at him from the side, swinging a deadly hand that took the man under the ear. There was a dry, sharp, snapping sound and the man went down and did not move again. Stark pulled the sword out from under his body.

No one else was in the temple, nor in the living quarters behind it. They found clothing, light loose things more suited to the climate than the off-world garments they wore, and far less conspicuous. Among these were wide hats of woven fiber, and sandals. In the kitchens they found food and took of it as much as they could carry, as well as knives and a flint-and-steel. They had no trouble finding a weapon for Ashton.

A path led from the temple compound toward the river. Following it, they came to a landing where one fine boat with a high, carved prow was moored in the place of honor and two battered old dugouts were drawn up on the bank. They left the fine boat to wait for the priests who would never come and pushed one of the dugouts into the brown water. It took them—a broad, strong current without haste.

They passed a few fishing villages, keeping always to the far side of the river. The villages were poor things and the fishermen seemed content to ignore them. Later in the afternoon, when they were in the middle of a wide reach, Stark heard a faraway faint sound and stiffened.

"Hoppers coming."

"What do we do, just carry on?"

"No. They would wonder why we weren't scared. Paddle like hell for the bank and don't lose your hat."

They paddled, churning a clumsy wake across the current.

The hoppers appeared from the west, high enough for the men in them to spot the villages and temple clearings they were looking for. They came over the river and then dropped suddenly, one behind the other, until they were almost on top of the dugout.

The downdraft hit. Stark and Ashton tumbled into the water, desperately holding the dugout to keep it from turning over and dumping everything they had.

Stark thought, They know us, they've recognized us in spite of the clothes . . .

But the hoppers, having had their little joke, swooped upward again and went their way east.

Stark and Ashton hauled themselves back into the dugout, and Ashton said, "I thought they had us."

"So did I. I wonder if they're Penkawr-Che's, or is there another ship closer by? The one that brought back Pedrallon."

"I don't know. But it's likely that ship would stay, if there are enough temples to loot."

Stark dug his paddle in. "We'll keep to the bank."

After a while he added, "If there is a ship, and if we can get to Pedrallon while it's still here, and if he's willing to help us, there might be something constructive we could do."

Ashton said nothing. He waited.

"When the hoppers are away raiding," Stark said, "and there's only a skeleton crew aboard, a strong force might capture the ship and hold it long enough for us to use the deep-space communications center. It's the only hope I can see now of getting us off this planet."

"Then, let us try. Anything at all."

They sent the dugout flying.

The hoppers crossed the river again at sunset, high and heading west.

Under the shadow of the bank, Stark smiled and said, "They're not Penkawr-Che's."

Hope took them down the river faster than the current.

11

In the House of the Mother, deep under the icy sparkle of the Witchfires in the far north, Kell à Marg, Skaith-Daughter, sat on the knees of the Mother and heard what her chief Diviner had seen in the great crystal Eye.

"Blood, yes," he said. "Blood, as we have seen before. Because of the off-worlder Stark, the House will be violated and some few will die. But that is not the worst."

Kell à Marg's body was slim and proud. Her white fur gleamed against the brown stone of the Mother's breast. Her eyes were large and dark, shining in the pearly light of the lamps.

"Let us hear the worst, then."

"The Mother's heartbeat slows," said the Diviner, "and the Dark Goddess moves. She is shod with ice and her mouth breathes silence. My lord Darkness walks at her right hand, and at her left is their daughter Hunger, and where they walk all is desolation."

"They have always shared this realm with the Mother," said Kell à Marg, "since the time of the Wandering. But Mother Skaith will live as long as Old Sun lives."

"Her life draws in, as his does. Has Skaith-Daughter looked out from her high windows across the Plain of Worldheart?"

"Not since the burning of the Citadel. I hate the wind."

"It would be wiser if you did so, nevertheless."

Kell à Marg looked at her chief Diviner, but he did

not waver nor turn aside; and so she shrugged and rose from her high seat, stepping from between the Mother's arms. She called one of her sleek tiring-women to come and bring a cloak. No one else was in the hall. The Diviner had wished to give her his heavy news in private.

They walked, Kell à Marg and the Diviner and the tiring-woman, through the long corridors and winding ways of the House of the Mother, past a hundred doorways into a hundred chambers filled with the relics of vanished cities and dead races. The quiet air smelled of dust and the sweet oil of the lamps, and it smelled of time also. The labyrinth extended upward and downward and on all sides through the mountain heart, the life work of this mutant race that had turned its back deliberately to the sky. Now there were so few of the Children left that a large part of the labyrinth was abandoned, with all its treasures, to the eternal dark.

A small coldness touched Skaith-Daughter, the veriest fingertip of fear.

At length they came into a corridor where there was nothing but bare stone and a bitter draft that bent the lamp flames, and at the far end an arch of light. Kell à Marg took the cloak about her shoulders and went ahead alone.

The arch gave onto a narrow balcony, a falcon's perch far below the peaks of the Witchfires that glittered against the sky, but high above the Plain of Worldheart. Kell à Marg's body flinched from the cruelty of the wind. Hugging the cloak about her, she leaned against the rock by the high parapet and looked out across the plain.

At first, she could see nothing but the glare of Old Sun and the blinding pallor of snow, shaping a dreadful emptiness. But as she forced herself to endure this ordeal, she was able to make out details. She could see where the Harsenyi road used to run, safe from the guardian Northhounds. She could see where the permanent camp of the Harsenyi had been, from which they had served the Lords Protector and such Wandsmen as had need of them on their comings and goings to the Citadel and among the dark settlements of the High North. She could see the vast, white emptiness of the plain and the wall of the Bleak Mountains beyond it; there the Northhounds had once ranged, before the man Stark had managed somehow to subdue them to his alien will.

She could not detect that anything had greatly changed. Seasons meant nothing to her, safe in the gentle womb of the Mother, but she knew that summer was a brief and stunted interval between one winter and the next, and that even in summer there was always snow. Summer, plainly, had come and gone; nevertheless, this winter that she looked upon seemed no different than any other. The cold might be more intense, the snow deeper, but she could not be sure. The wind skirled snow-devils across the plain, mingled with plumes of steam that spurted from the Thermal Pits, so that it was difficult to tell which was snow and which was steam. Beyond the pits, on the flank of the Bleak Mountains and invisible behind its eternal curtain of mist, would be the ruins of the Citadel. Because of that mist she had never seen the Citadel—only the smoke and flame of its burning.

But she saw it now.

She saw the ruins, black and broken, through the new thinness of the mist.

It frightened her. She pressed against the parapet, studying with a new intensity the action of the fumaroles. And it seemed to her that all across the thermal field the plumes of steam were scanter than she remembered, their spurting less frequent. That same thermal field underlay the House of the Mother. The food supply depended upon its warmth and moisture. If it should grow cold, all those who dwelt within the House must perish.

Great black clouds moved over the face of Old Sun. The light dimmed. The first veils of snow began to fall on the distant peaks.

Kell à Marg shivered and left the balcony.

She did not speak until they had gone from that corridor to another place that was free from draft and where the lamp flames were burning upright, and even then she kept the cloak about her.

She sent the tiring-woman away and said to the Diviner, "How long?"

"I cannot tell you, Skaith-Daughter. Only that the end is there, and that the Mother has given you a choice."

Kell à Marg knew what that choice was, but she made him put it into words, nonetheless, in case his wisdom might be greater than hers.

"We must go back into the world and seek another place, or else stay here and prepare to die. That may take some generations, but the decision cannot wait. When the Dark Goddess establishes her rule, there will be no second choice."

Kell à Marg drew the cloak still more closely about her, and still she was cold.

On the other side of the Witchfires, below the pass of the Leaning Man, the Ironmaster of Thyra cast his own auguries. He did this in private, with only his First Apprentice to assist him, in the forge that was sacred to Strayer of the Forges. This forge was set well into the towering flank of the ruin-mound where the men of Thyra burrowed and labored and brought forth iron pigs.

From the small furnace he took a little crucible of molten metal, and while the apprentice chanted the proper words he tipped the contents of the crucible into an iron basin filled with fine sand and cold water. A tremendous steam arose, and a wild bubbling, and when all that had gone the apprentice dipped away what water was left and the Ironmaster looked at the pattern that had formed on the sand.

Looked, and crossed his hands upon the great iron pectoral he wore that was wrought in the shape of Strayer's Hammer, and bowed his head. "It is the same. There is no health in the metal. The divine strength of

Strayer is gone from us."

"Will you try again, Ironmaster?"

"There is no use. We have the word of Strayer, he will not alter it. Look you. These small bright rills pointing south. Always south. But here to the north, again, the metal is twisted and dark."

The apprentice whispered, "Must we then leave Thyra?"

"*We* may stay," said the Ironmaster. "That choice is ours. But Strayer has gone before us. His quality is heat, the fire of the forges. He has fled before my lady Cold."

Southward from Thyra on the edge of the Darklands, the People of the Towers prepared themselves for winter.

The summer, always a blighted season, had been abnormally short and chill, so that the lichen-gatherers had been driven in early with a scant harvest and the hardy grasses had never come to seed. The People had faced bad winters before in their fortress-camp, where the broken towers stood around a wide circle with a faceless monument at its center. But never, they thought, had a winter come so soon as this one—with such terrible winds—and never had their beasts and their larders been so lean.

Hargoth the Corn-King and his sorcerer-priests, all narrow gray men with gray masks to cover their narrow faces from the cold, took up their ritual position. Hargoth, who worshiped the Dark Goddess but also fed Old Sun, maintaining a precarious balance between the two, spoke with his Lady. When this was done, he was silent for a long while.

Then he said, "I will cast the finger-bones of the Spring Child."

He cast them, three times, and three times, and three times.

Only Hargoth's eyes and mouth were visible behind his mask, which was marked with the stylized symbols of corn ears in a place where no corn had grown for a thousand years. Hargoth's eyes glittered and were bright with a light of madness that comes from the winter dark. His mouth spoke in jets of white vapor that blew away on the wind.

"They point south," he said. "Three times, and three times, and yet three times again. That way lies life and Old Sun. Here lies death and the rule of the Goddess. We must decide now which of them we shall choose."

He lifted his gaze to the remote and mocking sky and cried out, "Where is our Deliverer, the star-born one who was to lead us to a better world?"

"He was a false prophet," said one of the priests who had followed Stark and Hargoth to Thyra, and survived. "The ships are gone from Skaith. The star-roads are closed to us, as they have always been."

Hargoth walked toward the Towers, where his people dwelt. Beside the monument he paused and said, "For us they are closed, but perhaps they may open for our children, or for their children. And any life is better than death."

Again he cast the finger-bones. And again they pointed south.

12

Alderyk the Fallarin perched on a rock, looking at the view and disliking it intensely.

Accustomed as he was, for a lifetime, to the cold clean northern desert, he found the steamy air of these lowlands difficult to breathe, the over-active vegetation both wasteful and repulsive. Things grew on each other's backs, so that a plant was forced under and beginning to rot almost before it ripened. A sticky, green stench always filled his nostrils, and what time his fine dark fur was not being drenched by sudden rains it was dripping disgustingly with his own sweat.

Now, stretched out before him and running away over the rim of the world, was a heaving unpleasantness called the sea.

Beside him, his friend Vaybars said, "I think perhaps we made a mistake when we decided to follow the wise woman."

Alderyk grunted, and fingered the place at his neck where his gold torque had been before he gave it to Penkawr-Che as part of Vaybars's ransom.

"At least," he said, "we're doing one thing we set out to do when we came south. We're learning a lot about this wretched world we live on."

The mercenary had led them well, after one mistake. He had attempted to betray them by leading them to a town where there was a force sufficient to overwhelm them. Gerd had stopped that, and the hounds had given the man a lesson in the folly of trying to outsmart a pack of telepaths. He had not tried again.

He had brought them by rough and relatively untraveled ways, where the only people they met were vagabonds, or armed peasants who shut themselves up in their villages and watched them pass but did nothing to hinder them, except to charge enormous prices for food, which they bartered over their walls.

Even so, the party could not have got through without the hounds. Bands of mercenaries were quartering the country, searching for them. More than once they had hidden in a wood to watch a mounted troop go jingling by, or turned aside from their chosen direction to take a roundabout way because the hounds warned them of men ahead. All of one long night they had played cat-and-mouse with a mounted band in the defiles of some jungle hills—men they never saw and only managed to avoid because of the hounds.

Now, at last, they had reached the sea; and had discovered a particularly nasty village plastered to the cliffs below the place where the Fallarin perched. Tiny round houses, whitened with the droppings of a million flying things until they looked like lumps of guano, clung to the naked rock on both sides of a narrow cleft, climbing up from a little harbor on a series of shallow steps. At the foot of the steps, on the harbor side, was a minute inn that looked villainous even though Alderyk could see nothing of it but its peaked roof. He was not versed in the lore of harbors, but this one seemed adequately deep and was sheltered by a curving mole. Only one thing was visibly wrong with it: it had no boats.

Alderyk spread his wings wider. A damp and sluggish breeze was moving inward from the sea. He caught it in his wings and it pressed against him, ruffling his fur. It smelled of salt and fishy things. It was a lazy breeze, and stupid, but it could talk. He stroked it, and listened.

Vaybars, beside him, was doing the same thing. So were the four other Fallarin, strung out along the cliff wherever their fancy took them. The breeze talked to them all, glad of the company; small, soft, indolent talk, in which they could hear the lapping of water against hollow hulls, the slatting of idle sails and slack cordage.

From a little distance, Halk watched them and waited with scant patience.

The rest of the party, concealed in the fringes of the jungle that grew almost to the cliff edge, lay and eased their weary bones—all but Tuchvar, who fussed with the hounds.

The tropic heat made the Northhounds miserable, and there had been a lack of proper food. Tuchvar caressed their coats and told them how all would be well as soon as they were at sea aboard the boat. *Boat* was an entirely strange concept to them. *Sea* they had looked at and sniffed at from the edge of the cliff, and they had not liked it.

Gerrith sat beside Halk, her eyes closed, her hands lax. Perhaps she slept. Perhaps she saw things behind or beyond the closed lids.

Halk had been reared, in the ancient tradition of his city-state, to regard the wise woman of Irnan as an infallible oracle, or at least one to be taken very seriously. He had done so in regard to the prophecy of the Dark Man made by Gerrith's mother, and in spite of his doubts and bitter despair the Citadel of the Lords Protector had fallen, the siege of Irnan had been lifted, and the gates of the stars had been opened —almost. Almost. Which was worse than not at all, so that the prophecy had at last been proved false, a waste of labor and bloodshed and dying. Now *this* Gerrith had prophesied, and he could neither quite deny that prophecy nor quite believe in it. If the mantle of truth had descended upon Gerrith's shoulders, and there was still a chance that Irnan might be freed from the tyranny of Mother Skaith and her Lords Protector, then he must do all within his power to bring about that end.

On the other hand, Gerrith was a woman in love with a man, and who could say how much that love might color her visions?

Holding his sword across his knees, Halk polished the long blade with a bit of silk and thought about his shield-mate Breca, and how she had died with Thyra's cold iron in her belly, and how the Thyrans had tossed her to the Outdwellers as one tosses offal to hungry dogs.

Stark had led them to Thyra. Another man might have found a better way to the Citadel. He, Halk, might have found a better way, if the prophecy had named him as the savior of Irnan—and why not he, rather than a stranger, an alien outsider from the gods-knew-where among the stars? This had rankled in him from the beginning, so that he was torn between a desire for Stark to succeed because of Irnan, and a desire for Stark to be defeated because he had no right to be what he was. He blamed Stark for Breca's death. He had wanted a hundred times to kill him, and each time had been forced to stay his hand for the sake of Irnan.

This time, if the prophecy was false and Stark should fail again, nothing but the death of one of them would save Stark from the weight of this blade.

Gerd lifted his head and growled, taking the thought from Halk's mind, and Halk glared back into the demon eyes and said, *Not even you, hellhound. If Stark can withstand you, so can I.* And he ran his thumb along the cutting edge.

Alderyk came in from the cliff.

"There are boats," he said. "Mostly small, but one is big enough for us."

"Where is this boat?"

Alderyk gestured vaguely. "Out, with the small ones. It leads them. They're on some kind of hunt."

"Fishing."

"Very well, fishing. They will not return to the harbor before nightfall."

Gerrith said, "Ours must return now." She opened her eyes and looked at Alderyk and said again, "Now."

"We are too few to call great tempests," Alderyk said. "But we will do what we may."

He returned to the cliff. The six Fallarin went apart

and gathered themselves into a close group, with the Tarf standing guard about them. They spread their wings, gleaming red-brown in the sunlight, and began to sing to the little breeze that blew so soft and sluggish from the sea.

Halk could barely hear the song, but it had a quality of command, a compelling insistence that stirred deep wellsprings somewhere within his unimaginative soul. He disliked the Fallarin, as he disliked most things that forced him to stretch his mind a little wider. His passionate attachment to the cause of emigration had been purely pragmatic, based upon hatred of the slave's life his people led under the Wandsmen and the belief that life somewhere else would be better. His desire for the star-roads had held nothing of wonder. When he thought of the actual physical business of taking himself bodily to another world, he was filled with loathing.

Now he could not repress a slight shudder as the breeze began to strengthen.

Out at sea, beyond a jutting headland to the south, the fishing fleet felt a change. It was slight at first. The folk in the small boats, spread out with weighted nets dragging between them, did not notice it at all.

On the large boat, pride and protector of the fleet, the rowers snored on their benches and the master and his mate played languidly at dice beneath an awning.

The boat was designed for a twofold use—as a fighting ship to defend the fleet from marauders, human and otherwise, and as a transport ship to move the catch to market. Like most compromises, she left much to be desired in both departments. Still, she floated. She carried her own little skiff, and she had a splendid figurehead in the shape of a guardian spirit, who fronted the waves so defiantly that she appeared to have a rudder at both ends.

The big lugsail, which had been flapping listless as a bedsheet in the light breeze, began to fill. The yard swung. Cordage snapped taut, rattling through the blocks.

The master took a long pull at a stone bottle and considered whether he ought to rouse the crew and go through the tiresome business of lowering the sail—which would mean that it must then be raised again later on, an even more tiresome business. He decided to wait. The breeze might drop again. If it did not, he could simply slack off on the tackle.

The breeze did not drop. It became a wind.

The boat began to move.

The master shouted. The crew roused up. The rowers woke.

The wind was like a great peremptory hand, pushing. They could see the mark of it across the water, a cat's-paw a mile long and straight as an arrow, riffled with whitecaps. They looked at it and were terrified, because it was aimed solely at them and did not so much as brush even one of the small craft.

The boat quickened. Her thick mast creaked with strain. White water began to break beneath her heavy forefoot.

Master and crew cried out upon the Sea-Our-Mother and rushed to get the sail down.

The wind split itself into whips and clubs and drove them off the deck, to cower in the fishy stink below. Rowers struggled with their sweeps and were knocked from the benches. Like a demented thing the boat galloped through the water, flinging up spray and burying the guardian figurehead above his pride.

The fisher folk sat in their small craft with their nets, in a calm sea, watching their flagship rush away in the grip of the eerie wind. They watched the long, wild cat's-paw follow on behind, so that all the sea was still again after it had passed. They cried out very loudly to the Sea-Our-Mother, and at each other. Then they hauled in their nets, dumping what catch they had as an offering, and began to row quickly for the nearest shore.

On the cliff above the harbor, Halk and Gerrith looked out to sea. The wind whipped their clothing and tossed their hair. Away to their left the Fallarin continued to sing their hypnotic, commanding song, beating their wings to the cadence.

The boat came in sight around the headland, with its pregnant sail and its wake of whitecaps.

It set straight in for the harbor, and Halk warned furiously, "If they're not careful, they'll pile her onto the mole."

Below, in the village, someone shouted. People ran from the houses, an ill-favored folk, and dirty, for all they wore ornaments of sea-pearls. They stood on the harbor steps and stared, their voices rising shrill like the clatter of seabirds disturbed in their nesting place.

The wind quirked and shifted, sending the boat staggering safely into harbor.

The Fallarin ceased their singing. Their wings closed. The wind dropped. The boat drifted peacefully. A straggle of oars began to splash, working her into the mooring place by the mole.

The villagers began to stream down the steps. Men ran out along the mole to catch the mooring lines. The boat was made fast.

"Now," said Halk, and the company went down into the cleft, leaving the riding animals behind. The Northhounds led the way. They came to the topmost of the wide steps that made the village street, and went down between the ugly little houses that stank of guano and old fish and less fragrant things.

Some time before they reached the mole, the villagers forgot the ship and the strangeness of the wind, and made a great confusion of screaming and scattering, of rushing and hiding, away from the terrible hounds and the winged men and the not-men and the cloaked men and the men with bright swords.

No one hindered these from boarding the boat.

They cast off and worked her—painfully, for none of them had ever handled oars before—into open water, while the master and the crew watched openmouthed from the mole or splashed in the water where they had taken refuge overside.

Gerrith spoke to the Fallarin. "Take us south, my lords, as swiftly as your winds can blow," she said, and her face was white as bone. "They have almost reached the sea."

13

The river had widened, spreading itself into a number of channels running between muddy islands. There were more villages and more traffic. Stark and Ashton had managed to stay with the main channel by watching where the bulk of the traffic went and following it. They kept as far away as possible from other craft, and no one had paid them much attention, but by midday the river had become busy enough that they decided to haul out on one of the islands and wait for quieter times.

"There should be a town ahead somewhere," Ashton said. "Probably at the mouth of the river. We need a proper boat. This hollow log will never get us down the coast."

When Old Sun had gone to his rest, they set out again, in the brief darkness before the rising of the first cluster. The brown water, black now with a glimmer of stars in it, carried them smoothly. Here and there were boats with lanterns in their bows, where men caught whatever moved by night. Villages were scattered along the bank and on some of the larger islands. The smoke of cooking fires lay in bands across the water, and the sounds of voices came to them, and the evening cries of animals.

The dugout rounded a bend and suddenly there was nothing—no fishermen, no villages, no lights, no sounds. The men drifted in the silence, wondering.

The smell of salt water mingled with the river smell, and presently Stark could see an opening-out of the darkness ahead, marked by a spreading fan of turbulence where the rush of the river was blocked by the immovable mass of the sea.

At the very end of the jungle bank, a black bulk loomed very strangely against the stars.

"There's no town," said Ashton. "Nothing."

"That looks like a temple," Stark said. "Perhaps this is all sacred ground."

Ashton swore. "I counted on a town. We must have a boat, Eric!"

"There may be boats at the temple. And Simon, keep a sharp eye ahead."

"Something wrong?"

"There is always something wrong on Skaith."

Stark laid the heavy sword ready to hand and made sure the knife at his belt was free. The thick, wet smells of jungle and water imparted nothing to him but their presence, and yet behind them, under them, through them, subliminally, he sensed a faint rankness that stirred his memory and set the hairs prickling at the back of his neck.

The current slowed as it met the sea, but turbulence tossed the dugout roughly. They paddled in toward the bank.

"Lights," said Ashton.

The jungle had thinned. They could see the whole of the huge structure at the land's end. Low down in it were openings where pale lights glimmered. High above, shadowy pinnacles leaned crazily like the masts of a stranded ship, and Stark realized that part of the temple had sunk down and broken away, tilting toward the sea, toward the white water that quarreled and foamed.

He looked at that white water because he could see now that things moved in it, dark bodies leaping, rolling, frolicking. And he knew why this final stretch of the river was deserted.

Ashton was searching the bank. "I see a landing, Eric, and boats—two boats."

"Never mind," said Stark. "Get ashore."

He dug his paddle deep, fairly lifting the dugout with each stroke.

Ashton did not question. He bent his shoulders to it. Spray broke over them, soaked them to the skin, filled the bottom of the dugout. The bank was low and bare above the temple landing, but the jungle offered cover not too far away.

If they could just get ashore, if they could run for it—

The dugout went over as suddenly as if it had struck a rock.

It was pitch black under the water, which was filled with a great boiling and thrusting of powerful bodies. Stark fought his way to the surface and saw Ashton's face not ten feet away. He lunged toward it, drawing the knife from his belt.

Ashton vanished with a strangled cry.

Other heads appeared in a bobbing circle. They were earless and smooth as the heads of seals, with vestigial noses and the mouths of predators. They looked at Stark with eyes like pearls and they laughed, these bestial Children of the Sea-Our-Mother, with a dreadful echo of lost humanity.

Stark dived and swam, blindly, furiously, searching for Ashton and knowing that he was not going to find him. The creatures played with him. He was a strong swimmer, but they were better, and there were many of them. And he could not reach them with the knife. They let him up to breathe three times, and they let him see Ashton again, flung up bodily out of the water, still alive. Then he saw nothing more. Webbed and taloned fingers pulled him under. He lost the knife.

He had once killed a Child of the Sea with his bare hands. Now he tried to do it again, in the roiling dark, grasping at slick-furred bodies that slipped effortlessly away, until his lungs were bursting and the darkness had turned red behind his eyes. This time they did not let him up to breathe.

He came to lying on hard stone, vomiting water.

For a while all he could think of was the need to get

air into his lungs. When he was finished strangling and could think again, he saw that he was on the temple landing and that Ashton was retching in a puddle a few feet away while a man in a blue robe pounded on his back. The mutant Children of the Sea-Our-Mother, to the number of a dozen, crouched along the landing, their fur streaming.

More men in blue robes came from the temple; some of them bore torches. The first of the Three Ladies had risen, so that it was light enough to see by. There was something peculiar about the blue-robes—priests or monks as they might be—something brutish. They shambled in their gait, and their shaven heads showed curious shapes.

Ashton was breathing again and the man ceased to pound on him, turning to Stark. His eyes were like the eyes of the Children, milky pearls, and his hands had webs between the taloned fingers.

"You are off-worlders," he said. "You robbed our temple."

"Not we," Stark insisted. "Other men." His limbs felt heavy and his body was a hollow shell. Nevertheless, he gathered himself, looking at Ashton. "Why did the Children not kill us?"

"All who come this way belong to the Mother and must be shared with her. As you will be shared."

His speech was thick because of the shape of his lips and teeth. He smiled, and it was not a pleasant smile, with the dog teeth sharp and shining.

"You wish to run, off-worlder? Try. You have two choices—the water, or the land. Which will it be?"

The Children dripped, laughing, on the stones between Stark and the river. Several of the monks had produced long, thin tubes of carved ivory from beneath their gowns, and the tubes were pointed at Stark. Ivory, wood, or metal, and ornamented or not, a blowgun was a blowgun wherever you found it, and blowguns shot ugly little darts, generally poisoned.

"It is a safe drug," said the blue-robe. "You will be

alive and conscious when the Children share you—for
the greater pleasure of the Mother."

Stark measured his chances of breaking through
forty monks unscathed, and decided they were thin. In
any case, he could not take Ashton. If he did escape,
he might or might not be able to come back and rescue
his foster-father. But if he got himself knocked out by
a drugged dart, there would be no possibility of escape
for either of them.

He remained where he was, and did not protest when
a monk with a human face and no ears came to bind
his hands.

"What are you?" he asked the blue-robe. "Hybrids?
Throwbacks? The Children's blood is in you."

With a proud humility the man answered, "We are
the few whom the Mother chooses to be her special
servants. We are the sea-born who must live on land,
to keep the Mother's temple."

In other words, Stark thought, the odd births where
the mutation did not quite breed true.

"Your temple was robbed?"

"By men like you, who are not of Skaith. They
came from the sky with much noise and terrible lightnings. We could not fight them."

"You could have died trying. I know of priests who
did."

"What would have been the point of that?" asked
the blue-robe. "We lived, to pray for revenge." He
looked from Stark to Ashton, who was on his feet now,
and bound. "Only two of you. But perhaps you are a
token, a sign from the Mother that there will be more."

Stark said, "Those men are *our* enemies, too. They
tried to kill us. If you will help us to get south to
Andapell, we can find means to punish them, perhaps
even get back for you what they stole."

The blue-robe gave him a flat stare of utter contempt.
Then he glanced at the sky, judging the time that was
left until morning, and said to his fellows, "Let us
begin the preparation now. We will hold the feast at
dawn."

The path to the temple was broad and easy of ascent, even to bound men. The vastness of the building became apparent, its crushing bulk looming in the cluster light, rising to fantastic pinnacles all carved with the twisting shapes of sea-things.

It had many wings below. Stark and Ashton were taken into one of these, into a stone chamber where candles burned; and there the monks drugged them, anyway, by means of sharp slivers dipped in some pale liquid and driven beneath the skin.

Stark's battle was quickly over. He went from there fully conscious, seeing, hearing, and gentle as a lamb.

The night was not unpleasant. It had nothing in it of threat or danger to rouse alarm. The odd-looking men in the blue robes treated them kindly, even royally, though some of the praying was over-long and Stark slept. Otherwise, he was interested in what went on.

He and Simon were bathed in great sunken tanks of seawater, both hot and cold. The tanks were beautifully carved around their sides, and a great deal of ceremony was connected with the bathing. When it was finished, the men were dried with silken towels and their bodies were rubbed with various oils and essences, some of which smelled rather strange. Then they were wrapped in silken robes and brought to a chamber with many candles, where there was a place to sit down among soft cushions. Here they were fed a meal, a most peculiar meal of little separate dishes, each one with a different spice or savor.

In some dim, remote corner of his mind Stark felt that a few of the dishes ought to have been revolting to him, but they were not. From time to time Ashton would look at him and smile.

The remarkable thing about that whole period was that it had no edges or corners. All was rounded and smooth and easy. The night flowed sweetly, and just when the bathing and the feeding and the praying and the sleeping had begun to pall, the blue-robed men raised them and brought them by long corridors into the body of the temple.

They entered from the landward side, and it was like standing in the hold of some mighty ship that had broken its back on a reef, leaving the stern half untouched while the forward half tilted toward destruction. Looking upward into the shadowy dimness where the torch- and candlelight did not reach, Stark saw a great gash of open sky beyond a ragged edge where the vault ended.

The sky held the first faint hint of dawn.

The blue-robed men led them on, to where the blocks of the floor had drawn apart, one side level, the other raised at an angle. A way had been made across that gap, a kind of bridge, and they walked under the sky into the forward part of the temple.

Here they saw a blaze of candles, which showed the lower parts of reliefs on the walls, cracked and stained with dampness. The floor was much disarrayed, with blocks at all heights, and all running downhill to the front, where the entire wall had fallen and let in the sea. Wavelets lapped softly there with the candlelight shimmering on them. At one side, a platform built of the fallen stones projected into the water.

Centrally in this half-sunken hall, tilted crazily on her massive base, the Sea-Our-Mother rose up in whitest marble, twenty feet or more to the top of her crowned head, from a surging of marble waves about her waist. She had two faces. One was the bountiful mother who gives life and plenty, the other the destroying goddess who ravages and kills. Her right hand held fish and garlands and a tiny ship. Her left held wrecked hulls and sea wrack and the bodies of drowned men.

She had no other ornaments. Wrists and throat and the whiteness above her breasts were scarred with cruel pits; and her eyes, which had been jewels, were blind.

Stark and Ashton were made to stand before her. Their silken robes were removed. Monks brought garlands of sea-flowers and shells and twining weeds to hang about their necks. They were chill and wet against Stark's naked skin, and the smell of them was strong.

For the first time, a small worm of alarm began to eat away at his mild content.

A huge deep drum boomed in the temple, three times. Iron cymbals clashed. The monks began to chant, in growling basses that sounded against the vault as though great dogs barked in a cave, groaning out their most profound rage and misery.

Stark looked up at the vandalized faces of the goddess leaning above him. Fear shot through him, a cold spear stabbing him awake. But he could not quite remember what it was that he feared.

The monks had gathered round. They began to move, with Stark and Ashton in their midst, toward the water; and Stark could see that one of the blue-robes had come out onto the platform that jutted into the sea. He held a horn much greater than his own height in length, so that its curved end rested on the stone.

Drum and cymbals broke the growling chant with a blow of fierce emphasis, and the voices all together held one long, grinding note that was like the dragging of a boulder over rock.

It ended and the horn spoke, shouting a wild, hoarse, moaning cry out across the sea.

Ashton walked slowly beside Stark. He smiled vaguely and his eyes were untroubled.

They walked on the submerged floor, the water rising around their ankles, toward the place where the blue-robe stood with his sounding horn. They walked to the measured cadence of the chant and to the drum-beat and the cymbal clash, toward steps that rose out of trailing weed and the encrusting shells of small things that live in shallows. The sky had grown brighter and the candles turned pale.

The horn called, hoarsely, yearning, and the surface of the sea, which stretched like satin beneath the sunrise, was broken by the splashing of many swimmers.

Stark remembered what it was that he feared.

A cauldron of molten brass tipped out of the east. The burning light ran across the surface of the water. It caught in the sail of a boat going heavily before a wind that seemed to blow only for her, since all around her was a flat calm. It turned the sail to gold and the clumsy hull to a thing of loveliness.

It caught in the eyes of a white hound standing in the bows, and these flamed with a sudden brilliance.

N'Chaka, said Gerd. *N'Chaka! There! Danger. Things come.*

Kill? asked Tuchvar.

The canted spires of the temple burned in the distance. The voice of the horn came faintly across the sea.

Too far, said Gerd. *Too far.*

14

Stark was halfway up the steps. Blue-robes were in front of him, and on either side, and behind. They were absorbed in their chanting. Victims customarily went smiling to their deaths. Only at the very end, when they had been cast into the sea and the Children had begun to share them, were there cries amid the blood and the floating garlands; and both cries and blood were pleasing to the Mother. The monks sang in their growling voices and did not notice that Stark had ceased to smile.

He was still beyond any rational thought. He only knew that death was coming swiftly through the silken water to claim him. The life within him stirred—a simple, uncomplicated force that rose of itself to fight against extinction.

Ashton was at his right hand. At his left was a monk, and then a second monk, and then the unguarded edge of the steps.

Stark swung his left arm viciously. The blow took the nearer monk across the throat and swept him back into those who climbed behind him. In falling, he clutched at the second monk and cost him his balance. Blue-robes tumbled and fell, splashing into the shallow water. Stark rushed up out of the space he had opened, clearing more space ahead of him by knocking other monks into the water. Hands caught at him, tearing away the garlands but slipping on his naked, oiled body. Some of the fingers had talons that drew blood, but they could not stop him. He gained the platform with a wild bull's rush.

The blue-robe with the horn turned about, startled. He had an especially brutish face. Stark took the horn from him. With it, he broke the face and sent the blue-robe flying out into the water on the far side of the platform. Then Stark swung the long horn like a ten-foot club to clear the upper steps.

He shouted, "Simon!"

Then he heard a faint voice calling his name, *N'Chaka, Man-Without-a-Tribe,* and he wondered who on this death-bitten godhaunted planet knew that name to call him. And suddenly he realized that the voice was in his mind, and he knew it and cried out, "Gerd!"

He said it aloud, and Simon Ashton looked up at him, vacant-eyed and smiling.

Gerd, kill!

Too far. Fight, N'Chaka.

Stark lashed about him with the long horn. It was made of metal, bound and bossed, and it was heavy. He roared for Simon Ashton to come to him, roared in English and in clicks and grunts.

The chanting had become chaotic. Some of the monks in the farther ranks still kept at it as the drum boomed and the cymbals clashed, but the monks up front were in confusion. Most had not yet realized what had happened. The long horn beat among them like the flail of the Lord, and Ashton, frowning in puzzlement, began to pick his way through the floundering bodies toward Stark.

The rear ranks of blue-robes put aside their chanting. They voiced a mingled cry of outrage and fury, and charged forward up the steps, trampling their fellows.

Stark caught Ashton's hand and dragged him up onto the platform.

Gerd, kill!

Too far, N'Chaka. Fight.

Stark fought, swinging his flail until it bent and broke and he flung it away. He took hold of Ashton and leaped with him into the water, on the seaward side of the platform, where the Children were coming to share their sacrificial meal with the Goddess.

The water was unexpectedly deep. The first monk he had thrust over was drowning in it.

Now that the horn had stopped its calling, the Children seemed to have paused. He could see their dark heads bobbing some fifty feet away. They hooted plaintively as though wondering what had happened to upset the ritual. There were a lot of them. Stark did not stop to count. Pulling Ashton, he swam out around the broken wall, heading toward the nearest land. Behind him, monks tore off their robes and sprang in after him.

As soon as he was clear of the temple, Stark saw the boat. It shot toward him, parallel to the shore, blown by a narrow gale that seemed in a fair way to drive it under.

The monks swam almost as agilely as their full-mutant brothers. The Children called in their subhuman voices, and the monks answered them. The Children came on again, swerving like a school of fish, heading straight for the escaping sacrifice.

Ashton was inclined to be querulous, as one might be when shaken roughly from a pleasant nap. He slowed Stark down considerably. When they scrambled out onto the muddy beach, the monks were so close behind that one had sunk his talons into Ashton's leg and was pulling him back.

Ashton came out of his tranquil dream.

He screamed and turned to fight. Stark got both hands under the monk's thick jaw and pulled sharply upward. There came a snapping sound and the monk let go of Ashton, who crawled away from him on all fours, trailing blood. Then he got up and ran.

Stark turned to run with him, but brutish bodies were hauling out all around him. Hands gripped his ankles. He bent to free them and other hands caught at him. Things leaped upon him and he fell, amid a great squattering and splashing, to roll in the tepid shallows with a weight of rancid fishy bodies on him.

Ashton picked up a stone and came back to crack heads with it.

Stark broke free. But they brought him down again by sheer weight, and Ashton with him. A purely animal sound came from Stark's throat, once. After that he fought in silence. A leathery paw came clawing for his face and he sank his teeth into it until they grated on bone. Blood was in his mouth, strange-tasting blood. The monk wrenched his hand away, shrieking. Then, suddenly, all the monks were shrieking. The blows stopped coming. The weight of bodies lessened. Those that remained became inert.

Stark pushed them off and got to his hands and knees.

Monks lay about on the mud, their dead faces contorted with terror. The boat was riding in flat calm now, off the shore. He could see the white heads of hounds along the rail.

We kill, N'Chaka. You come.

The Children of the Sea were not coming any closer. Some of them floated facedown in the water. Those who still could were thrashing away in a frenzy of speed.

Stark got up and helped Ashton to his feet, pointing to the boat. Neither man had any idea how it had come there. Neither man stopped to question. They walked into the sea until it deepened, and then they swam. Ropes were let down and powerful arms helped them aboard.

Stark was aware of faces, aware of voices shouting, aware of the hounds clustered round him, but the only thing that was really clear to him was the face of Gerrith. She came to him and he held her, and neither minded the blood and seawater that wetted them both.

"You live," she whispered. "Now the way is open." And he tasted salt on her lips that was sharper than all the salt of the sea.

The Fallarin perched on the deck, falcons in moult with their fur awry and their sullen eyes half mad with exhaustion.

"If *more* haste is needed," said Alderyk, looking at

the tribesmen and the Irnanese, "get you to the rowing benches. We are foredone." He bared his white teeth at Stark. "Show us wonders now, Dark Man. We have earned them."

Stark said, "I don't understand."

Gerrith stepped back. "Presently, the whole story. But you must have orders for us now. What are they?"

Stark put an arm around Gerd's neck, and the other around Grith's, and his mind touched the minds of all the hounds. He smiled at Tuchvar, and at Sabak and the tribesmen, who had shed their dusty cloaks but not their veils. The Irnanese he did not know, but he smiled at them. He even smiled at Halk.

"We go south to Andapell," he said. "We break our backs for Andapell, if the winds won't blow. Alderyk, loan us your Tarf. They can pull twice as well as we can."

He let go of the hounds and jumped down to the rowing benches. He was not tired now. His many wounds were slight and of no account. He looked at Halk and laughed.

"Surely you'll not stand by while the Dark Man rows? Come on, comrade. Bend your back for Irnan."

He thrust out the clumsy sweep and felt it bite. "Yarrod!" he shouted. "Yarrod! Yarrod!"

The Irnanese laid aside their arms and tumbled down to the benches, picking up the old battle-cry. "Yarrod! Yarrod!" They ran more oars out.

Halk put down his great longsword and sat on the bench beside Stark so that they worked one oar together. "Yarrod!"

The tribesmen, proud dainty riders of the cold desert, put their feet into the slopping bilges and rowed, side by side with the four-armed Tarf.

The oars dipped raggedly. They fouled each other and men cursed as the looms thumped them painfully. Gradually the stroke steadied, as the battle-cry became a chant; and they began to feel the rhythm, bending their backs in time.

The boat began to move forward.

The sea was unbroken, except for the turbulence where the river flowed into it. And nothing stirred there but the wavelets. The temple of the Sea-Our-Mother leaned wearily toward the water. In the full light of Old Sun its spires seemed very ancient, the carvings rubbed flat by the passing of centuries. No sound of drum or horn or cymbal came from the shadowed interior, nor was there any sound of voices.

The boat gathered speed, dropping south along the coast to Andapell.

15

Cereleng, chief seaport and capital of Andapell, sprawled across a circle of hills and down along the slopes to the harbor. The palace complex stood highest of all, gleaming white in the light of the Three Ladies, a gossamer fantasy of domes and arches and soaring pillars wrought in ivory and fretted marble.

The sailors' quarter stood lowest, a maze of lanes and streets, warehouses and shops and marketplaces, stretching in a wide crescent by the water's edge. The harbor was crowded with shipping, from the big round-ships of the deep-sea traders to little scuttling craft that shot like beetles among moored fishing boats and float-ing colonies of houseboats. Riding lights were a small galaxy of stars caught in the placid water.

Ashore, the streets were crowded with folk of all kinds. Seamen from half of Skaith mingled with the local inhabitants—smooth amber-skinned people wrapped in bright silks—and with darker, knottier little men from the interior, come down to trade with bark bundles of *tlun* and precious bits of worked ivory and wood and colored stone.

Others were here as well. The tropics were comfort-able in winter, and the seasonal migration of Farers was well along. Since food was come by with less effort here than in the north, there was less resentment among the people who produced it. Nevertheless, Wandsmen were present to see that the laws of the Lords Protector were kept. The Farers, in their infinite variety of hair, garments, paint, and nudity, strolled or lounged where they would, helping themselves from food stalls, chewing *tlun,* celebrating the end of their world with love and music and some really startling stenches.

Stark kept as wide of them as he could. He was clad as a wandering sailor, with his black hair clubbed at the back of his neck. He wore a loincloth with a knife stuck in it, and he carried a folded scrap of canvas over his shoulder to serve as cloak or bedding. His feet were bare and his expression stupid. He padded the dirty streets of the bazaars. He loitered around food stalls and drinking places. He bought nothing because he had no money. He listened, and avoided the Wandsmen.

Men carried on with their everyday lives and their bargaining and chaffering, but it was as though a heavy cloud hung over the quarter, so that even the flourishing sin shops were subdued and folk spoke in low voices over their wine.

Their talk was of two matters.

When he had heard enough, Stark returned to the beach where he had left the little skiff. Then he sculled out to where the boat had dropped her anchor stone in an open mooring, as far away from other craft as she could get. Cloud, with a flicker of lightning in it, had obscured the lowest of the Three Ladies. The air was oppressive, so that Stark sweated at his sculling.

The company waited under a jury-rigged awning that somewhat concealed them from curious eyes. Now that they had reached their goal, they were becoming peevish with confinement, and the hounds growled continually.

Ashton did not wait for Stark to get aboard. "The starship," he asked, leaning over the rail, "is it still here?"

"It is, somewhere." Stark made his painter fast to the rail and climbed over. "The town is all a-mutter with it, like a henroost with a fox about. They don't fear attack here, Cereleng is too large and well-defended. But every day fresh word comes in of temples plundered, villages robbed, people killed. The Wandsmen are busy spreading tales, so probably half of them are lies. But the ship is still here."

"Thank God for that," said Ashton. "We'll have to hurry. Where is Pedrallon?"

"That is the other thing they talk about. Pedrallon, and the ransom. They're not angry about the ransom. Honor required them to redeem their prince from the hands of the ungodly so that they can punish him properly themselves. They blame Pedrallon for intriguing with off-worlders. They say he ought to be fed to Old Sun."

"He has not been?"

"Not yet. But he's out of power, a prisoner in his own palace. His brother is now Prince of Andapell, and it's only a matter of time. And not very much of it!"

Ashton shook his head. "That's hard news. I had counted on Pedrallon's help."

"Must we worry about this Pedrallon?" Halk demanded. "If the starship is still here, and is necessary to us, let us go to it."

"I'd like to do that," Stark said, "but I don't know where it is."

"Couldn't you hear? Did no one say—?"

"Everyone said. Everyone knew. I saw men come to blows about it. No two places are the same. Some one of them is right, of course, but there's no way to tell which one that is, nor how to get there."

The clouds had reached higher, covering the second of the Three Ladies. It was much darker and thunder sounded in the west. The hounds grumbled, shifting uneasily in their places.

"Pedrallon would know," Stark said.

Halk made an angry gesture. "A pox on Pedrallon! Forget the ship. The wise woman says that our road leads south."

Stark said, "I can't forget the ship."

"What, then?" asked Ashton. "There are not enough of us to storm the palace."

Lightning flickered and flared, lacing the horizon. Stark said, "We won't leave harbor anyway, until that's past. I'll go up with Gerd and Grith. Perhaps we may arrange something. Be ready to move when you see us coming."

He let himself over the rail and called the hounds, not waiting for further argument. Making Gerd and Grith lie down in the bottom of the skiff, he sculled back to the shore, and thunderheads swallowed the last of the Three Ladies.

He beached the skiff at a place where unlighted warehouses clustered about a pier and where there was no one to see him. Hiding the skiff underneath the pier, he set off through furtive lanes toward the upper town, moving fast with the two hounds at his heels.

The houses here were mostly dwellings, shouldering together up the slope, redolent of sweat and spices. Only a few mean shops were open. What folk were abroad stared at the white hounds, but no one attempted to interfere.

By the time Stark had reached broader avenues, the first drops of rain were falling, great fat things that stung like hail, striking the paving stones far apart with a sharp splatting sound.

The rain ceased, and it became very dark in between the lightning. Thunder cracked the sky and made the ground tremble underfoot. Then rain came again, this time in torrents that swept the streets clean of all idle strollers.

The houses, which became larger and grander as Stark climbed, were set back in walled gardens. Heavy fragrances of unfamiliar flowers mingled with the smell of rain. Water rushed in the gutters.

The wall of the palace complex was high and white. At the main gate stood a gatehouse of marble, lovely as a jewel box, with lights in the windows and no sentries visible outside. The gate itself was barred shut. Stark passed it by. The wall was very long, girdling the hilltop in a huge irregular circle. He trotted beside it in the hammering downpour, the wet hounds flinching and groaning every time the sky split open.

Half a mile or so around, Stark came to a small gate,

heavily barred. He guessed that it served the kitchen quarters. Inside it was a sentry box with a porch where a huge gong was hung, presumably for the sounding of alarms. A lantern burned inside the open door.

Men, said Gerd. *There.*

Wait.

Stark drew back a little and then ran at the wall, leaping to catch the top with his fingers. He pulled himself up and over, dropping lightly on the other side. A flare of lightning showed him gardens, drenched and deserted, with white buildings beyond. The sentry box was at his left, about twenty feet away.

Kill, N'Chaka?

Not unless I tell you.

He went toward the small stone structure, not worrying too much about stealth. The storm would cover any sound he might make. Coming under the shelter of the porch, he found two men in scarlet—the palace color—kneeling on a mat in the small room, absorbed in a game that was played with dice and ivory counters. Perhaps they felt that there was no need to keep watch in this storm. Perhaps the present prince did not want too close a watch to be kept at all, in case a mob should roll up and relieve him of the embarrassment of his brother.

The men started up, seeing Stark. They cried out with one voice that was lost in a crash of thunder, and they reached for the weapons they had leaned against the wall.

Stark kicked the wind out of one of them, knocked the other hard against the stone, and then made sure they were both unconscious. He bound them carefully and gagged them with strips of scarlet silk.

Then he went and lifted the bars of the gate. The hounds rushed in.

Find Wandsman.

He put Pedrallon into their minds, not the name but the look of him. *Wandsman who came with N'Chaka.*
He put into their minds the time and place.

Remember Wandsman, they answered. They were
conditioned to remember Wandsmen.

Hurry. And watch.

They ran across dark lawns ankle-deep in water,
beneath bending trees turned silver by the lightning.
The palace buildings were enormous in extent, with
colonnades and domed pavilions lovely as pale dreams.

Too many minds there, N'Chaka.

Try.

The palace windows were dark, as though most of its
people slept. Only the guards' stations were lighted.
Stark kept away from those. The hounds would warn
him of patrols. But if there were any, they must have
been indoors somewhere, sheltering from the storm.

Too many minds. Sleep. Gray.

Try!

They passed long, marble wings that wandered
among fragrant gardens. They passed sunken court-
yards and pools. They found nothing.

Stark began to believe that it was a hopeless quest,
and not too bright a thought in the first place. He did
not care to be caught in the palace grounds when the
storm had passed. He was on the point of going back
when Gerd spoke suddenly.

Wandsman there!

Lead.

"There" was a small pavilion set apart from the
main mass of the palace. It was round, with graceful
arches and a spired roof, and no walls. Candles burned
in tall stands, the flames going straight up because in
spite of the storm there was little wind. In the center
of the marble floor a man knelt, his head bowed in an
attitude of contemplation. There was a stillness about
the kneeling figure, surrounded by brightness and seen
through a curtain of falling rain, which suggested that
the person who dwelt within it was faraway.

Stark recognized Pedrallon.

Four men stood around him with their backs to the
rain. They stood quite still, leaning on their spears,

watching him. No one else was nearby. The sleeping palace was quiet and remote.

Stark gave the hounds their orders.

The storm muffled sound, swallowed up the thin screaming of men in mortal terror. Stark and the hounds gained the platform of the pavilion and the men groveled on it. Stark moved swiftly among them, clubbing with the butt of a spear until they were all silent. Afterward, he bound them, working very fast.

Pedrallon had not risen from his knees. He wore only a white waistcloth, and his slender body might have been carved from amber, so motionless he held it. Only his head had lifted so that he might see Stark.

"Why do you disturb me?" he asked. "I am preparing for death."

"I have friends, and a boat in the harbor. You have no need to die."

"Because of my dealings with Penkawr-Che, I am responsible for what has happened," Pedrallon said. "I will not live with shame."

"Do you know where this ship is that preys on your people?"

"Yes."

"Could you lead us to it?"

"Yes."

"Then there is still hope. Come with me, Pedrallon."

The rain poured down, sheeting from the roof edges, though the candles burned steadily.

The hounds nosed and prowled among the fallen guards. *Hurry, N'Chaka.*

"What hope?" asked Pedrallon.

"Of bringing help, bringing ships and punishing Penkawr-Che—of saving the people who want to be saved. All the things you risked your life for." He looked down at Pedrallon. "Where is the man who was going to go on fighting the Wandsmen, no matter what?"

"Words. I am a captive under my own roof. I have no followers. My people scream for my blood, and my brother is in haste to satisfy them. Deeds, I have found, are more difficult than words."

His face was as Stark remembered it, a fine construction of aristocratic bones and smooth flesh, but the tremendous force that once had blazed in it was absent. The dark eyes that had burned with so much vitality were now cold and dull.

"You speak of things that concerned me yesterday, in another life. That time is gone."

Pedrallon bent his head again.

Stark said, "You will come with me now. If you do not, the hounds will touch you. Do you understand?"

Pedrallon did not stir.

The hounds touched him. They flogged him to his feet with little whips of terror. They drove him beside Stark out across the dark and streaming lawns.

"How long before someone comes to the pavilion?"

"No one comes," Pedrallon answered, sobbing, "until the guard is changed. I spend my nights and days there, fasting—"

"When is the guard changed?"

"When Old Sun rises."

Does he lie, Gerd?

No.

Does anyone follow?

They went the shortest way to the gate. The sentries were still quiet. Stark closed the gate behind them and set off down the hill. Pedrallon was beside him, heavy and stumbling, as though hunger had weakened him. Stark steadied him, his own ears stretched for any sound of alarm or pursuit behind them.

None came, nor did the hounds give any warning.

The storm rolled away slowly over the jungle. The rain slackened. It was very late now, and the few folk who prowled the swimming streets saw no more than a pair of sailors hurrying back to their ship.

Stark found the skiff where he had left it. Pedrallon sat in it with a hound front and back. Stark sculled out to the mooring.

Ready hands pulled them aboard, hoisted up the skiff

to its place on the deck. Rowers jumped to the benches. The sweeps ran out. The anchor stone came thumping up over the stern and the boat moved through glassy water, toward the open sea. Overhead, the clouds had broken, letting through rifts of silver light.

Pedrallon sat dazed and exhausted. Tuchvar brought wine and he drank it. It seemed to bring a little life back into him. He looked at the hounds and shuddered. He looked round at his shipmates, and made a gesture to Ashton, recognizing him. Then he turned to Stark.

"Is there truly hope?" he asked.

"I think so, if you lead us quickly to that ship."

"Well, then," Pedrallon said, "I will break my fast."

16

Old Sun was newly risen, but already it was hot. Lying in the fringe of the jungle, Stark could feel the runnels of sweat trickling on his naked back.

He was looking out from under a noisy canopy of trees where innumerable nameless creatures shouted and quarreled, going about the business of a new day.

He was looking at the starship.

Pedrallon had led them well since he woke from the drugged apathy of despair. The faint hope that he might yet defeat the Lords Protector and set his world free had been enough to kindle something of the old fire in him again. The sheer, vicious desire to strike a punishing blow against Penkawr-Che had done the rest.

By his direction, the Fallarin had given them a hurrying wind south, to a tiny inlet, where the boat was worked in under oars and concealed from passing ships and over-flying hoppers. The Fallarin remained, with the Tarf, to guard her and to gather strength. Pedrallon's enemies were not likely to accept his disappearance with equanimity, and once the pursuit was under way the fugitives would have to move fast to keep ahead of it.

In the breathless heat of noon, Pedrallon had brought the rest of the troop to a village. He had hunted these jungles many times, he said, and the man who had served him as guide and tracker knew every trail in this part of Andapell. He could take them directly to the ship.

"But will he serve you now?" asked Halk.

113

Stark glanced at the hounds, but Pedrallon shook his head. "You will not need them."

And they did not. Pedrallon entered the village and came back with a small, wiry man named Larg, who said that Pedrallon was his lord and his friend and that whatever Pedrallon wanted, he would do.

So they followed Larg, all that day and through the night, toward the place where Pedrallon had told him to go. They halted only to rest briefly and eat the hard rations they had brought with them. And all the way Stark was haunted by the fear that they were too late, that the ship had already gone to rendezvous with Penkawr-Che on the heath and that they were straining their hearts out for nothing.

It was not necessary to say this to Ashton. His anxious face mirrored the same fear.

They came at last, in the moonless morning time before Old Sun was up, to the edge of the jungle, and they saw the great towering shape gleaming faintly in the starshine and knew they were not too late.

The ship sat on a triangular plain of gravel laid down by the flooding of two small rivers, or by two branches of the same river, that came down over a rock wall in two separate waterfalls a quarter-mile apart to join again some distance below. This was not the flood season and the water was no more than ankle deep. It made a pleasant chuckling sound going over its stony bed. But Stark was not pleased by it. He saw the stream as an obstacle; not a large one, to be sure, but one he could have done without.

The ship was small by interstellar standards. Like *Arkeshti,* she was designed for use on the out-worlds, where port facilities were primitive or nonexistent. Small as she was, she bulked impressively on the plain, propped level on massive landing legs, her outer skin scored and pitted by alien atmospheres and the dust that drifts between the stars.

When Old Sun came up, Stark was able to see more detail than he had at first, and none of it was reassuring. Three hoppers squatted in a line close to the ship.

They were inside a perimeter guarded by three laser cannon on portable mounts. The cannon had their own power cells, and they were emplaced to cover all approaches to the open hatch of the ship. The two-man crews walked about or lounged between the canvas awnings that sheltered each emplacement.

"They run a tight ship," said Ashton, lying at Stark's left. "Without the hounds, I shouldn't care to face those cannon."

"My brother has not cared to, either," Pedrallon said. He was at Stark's right. "The Wandsmen impressed upon him the futility of an attack and he was only too eager to agree. The Wandsmen are pleased with the depredations because of the hatred they rouse against foreigners. They do not wish to have them stopped." He stared hungrily at the ship. "We must take her, Stark. If possible, we must destroy her."

Six men emerged from the ship. They spoke to the six men of the gun crews, who went up the ramp and inside—to get their breakfasts, Stark supposed, and then some sleep. The six newcomers took their places by the cannon.

Halk came up, from the place some distance away where the troop was resting, under orders to make no sound. He crouched down, glowering at the hoppers.

"Will they never take those damned things off?" he said.

"It's early yet."

"They must be near the end of their looting," Pedrallon said. "My brother has kept me supplied with each day's report of temples robbed and villages plundered. Even allowing for lies, Andapell must be nearly stripped, as well as the principalities that neighbor us."

"Let's hope the hoppers have one more day's work," Stark said. "If they open that cargo hatch to load the hoppers in, we'll have to hit them with all hands present, something I don't want to do."

"Surely," said Halk, "your Northhounds can carry all before them."

"The Northhounds are not immortal, and those are

powerful weapons. A tramp like this one draws hands from all over the galaxy, and some of them may be like the Tarf, immune to the hounds. If there are too many immunes, or if there's just one and he happens to be in charge of a cannon, we won't have such an easy time of it."

"Look," said Pedrallon.

More men were coming out of the ship. They walked toward the hoppers and began to check them out.

Ashton gave a sigh of relief. "They're leaving, then."

The men completed their ground inspection. Four climbed into each of the hoppers. The rest sauntered back toward the ship. Motors woke to life. One by one the hoppers lifted, droning into the sky.

"Good," said Stark. "Now we wait a while."

"Wait?" said Halk. "What for?"

"For the hoppers to get so far away that they can't come whipping back in five minutes when somebody yells to them on the radio."

"Radio!" Halk growled. "These off-world toys are a pest."

"No doubt," said Stark, "but think how many times, on our journey north and back again, you would have given all you possessed to know what was going on at Irnan."

Stark settled himself for the wait, drowsing like a cat in the growing heat.

Pedrallon and Simon Ashton discussed between them what radio message would be sent to Galactic Center if they did actually gain their objective. The discussion was not entirely amicable.

Finally Ashton got the official steel in his voice and eye, and said, "The message must be brief and readily understood. I can't give the history of Skaith in ten words. There is no guarantee that any message is going to be received at Pax in time to do any of us any good; but I can tell you that if they receive a request for an armada to interfere in a civil war on a non-member planet, they'll pretend they never heard it. I will identify myself and ask for a rescue ship. I will also state that Penkawr-Che and two other captains are up to no good here—and they can do what they want to about that. For us, one ship is enough and all we can hope for. You'll still have to go to Pax to plead your case."

Pedrallon gave in, without enthusiasm. "Where will you rendezvous? If the ship comes at all."

Ashton scowled. That point had been a major problem between himself and Stark. The fact was that they could not guarantee to be in any particular place for any length of time. They could not even guarantee to be alive.

Ashton answered, "There must be a portable transceiver aboard the ship."

"And if there isn't?"

"We'll make an alternative arrangement." And hope, Ashton thought, remembering the inhospitable vastness of the planet.

Old Sun rose higher. The heat became a physical thing, a weight that dragged down drooping branches and pressed on the bodies of men so that breathing became a conscious labor and hardly worth the effort. The gravel plain shimmered. The starship seemed to float above it. The gun crew dozed under their awnings.

All but one man.

He was short and round and his skin was grayish-green like the skin of a lizard. His head was naked and quite broad, with a ridiculously small face set in the middle of it. His birthworld circled a lusty young primary, so he was used to heat. He had not even bothered to open the collar of his tunic. He walked toward the stream, thinking of home and friends and calculating how much his share of the loot would come to.

The jungle stood like a green wall across the stream. It was very still. All the morning noises had died under the weight of approaching noon. The lizard man picked up a flat pebble and sent it skipping across the shallow water.

Inside the hatch, in the ship, it was cooler. Ventilators sucked and roared. The two men sitting in the open airlock were enjoying the breeze. They were relaxed and somnolent, eyes half closed against the swimming glare outside. They heard nothing but the ventilators; they did not expect to hear anything. They had heard nothing on any of the other days when they had been on guard here in this remote place. In any case, they were not worried. The people of Skaith had nothing with which to fight them.

Each of the two men had beside him a heavy automatic weapon. The hatch control was on the wall beside the opening. Their duty was to defend the hatch, activating the control if that should become necessary. They did not expect it to become necessary, and in fact they considered the duty superfluous, though they did not say so. At least it was comfortable. They could see the emplacements outside, baking in the sun, and were glad they were not in them.

They could see, also, that one of the men had gone down to the stream to skip stones. They thought he was crazy. But they did not understand it when he began suddenly to scream.

They saw him fall down, writhing in the water. Great white animals burst from the edge of the jungle and hurtled across the stream, jetting bright drops from under their paws.

Men came after them, running.

17

Water splashed on Stark's bare skin, hot from the sun. The rocks were warm and slippery beneath his feet. He watched the cannon through the flying spray, waiting for a lightning bolt that would sear them all into lumps of blackened flesh like the priests of the temple by the sacred grove.

Kill! he shouted to the hounds. *Kill!*

They were already doing that. The gun crews died very quickly in their pits, without touching the firing studs.

The hounds ran fast toward the open hatch.

A man fell outward from it, onto the ramp. He lay there, curled in a fetal ball with his arms over his head.

Other man, N'Chaka. Think harm.

Kill!

Not easy like others . . .

Stark ran across hot, dry gravel. He had forgotten the cannon. His gaze was fixed now on the open hatch. If it should be closed against them, they would have to try and blast it open with the cannon, but even if that were possible it would take too much time. If the remaining man in the lock should be an immune—

Kill!

The sound of a man screaming mingled with the sudden hammering of shots from the lock. Gravel flew in little spurts. Two of the hounds went awkwardly over their own heads and did not get up again.

The hatch remained open and there was no more sound.

Eleven hounds dashed up the ramp, spurning the dead man with their cat-clawed feet.

Kill!

Hound-minds sought through steel bulkheads, through strange distances reeking with the unfamiliar stinks of oil and metal. They sought man-minds. They sent fear.

Stark ran, and his breath was harsh in his throat. The sun beat down and the two white hounds lay bloody on the ground. Behind him, Halk and the tribesmen and the Irnanese were busy with the cannon. Gerrith, Pedrallon, and Simon Ashton followed Stark. Tuchvar had stopped by the dead hounds.

Stark ran up the ramp.

Inside the lock he heard no sound except the panting of the hounds. The second man, who had not been as easy to kill as the others—an alien with butter-colored skin and a very massive skull—lay contorted in death. He was still holding his weapon in short-fingered hands that looked more like paws. Stark took it from him.

The inner hatch was open. The short corridor beyond it was empty.

Men?

Yes. Gerd growled and the metal walls echoed menace.

Not kill?

Like Tarf. Not hear us.

Many?

One and one.

Where?

There.

"There" was up.

Gerd's mind pictured gray, hard, not friendly, not understand, dark things, bright things; the place where the men were, the place he could see through their eyes.

Men think harm, N'Chaka.

Watch.

Ashton came up the ramp, breathing hard. He paused to pick up the other automatic weapon. Gerrith came behind him. Her face gleamed with moisture. Pedrallon, at her side, was barely sweated. His eyes were bright, almost as savage as the hounds'.

"Two men are still living," Stark said. "The hounds can't touch them."

"Only two men?" Pedrallon said.

"Armed." Stark lifted the automatic. "There's no need for you to come."

Pedrallon shook his head. "I must come. This is my world."

Stark shrugged. He looked at Gerrith. "Stay here."

"As you wish," she said. "But this is not my death day, nor yours."

Outside, one of the cannon had been disabled by shearing the cable from its power cell with a battle ax. The tribesmen were struggling back across the stream with a second one. They would set it up under cover at the edge of the jungle, where they could rake the landing area in case the hoppers returned. The Irnanese were bringing the third one, to set it up inside the airlock. Both Halk and Sabak had learned the rudiments of handling a laser cannon during the time Stark had had the armed hopper at Irnan. Stark left them to it, and sent nine of the hounds back out to Tuchvar, keeping Gerd and Grith with him. He nodded to Ashton and Pedrallon, then they proceeded into the short corridor.

It was no use taking any more troops with them. They had only the two automatic weapons. Swordsmen in the narrow passages of the ship would be an encumbrance rather than a help. Stark wished that Pedrallon had stayed behind, but he could not deny the man's right to accompany them.

At the end of the corridor a round hatch gave onto the central well of the ship.

A small ship, as starships went. Yet from this angle it seemed enormous. Stark looked up and still up, past

the various levels that contained the drive rooms, both
conventional and hyperdrive; the heavy reactors that
powered them; the cargo holds and life-support systems
and storage rooms. The cylindrical walls tapered toward the nose, to living quarters and the bridge.

Up there, at the very top—along with the control
systems, the computers, and the navigation tank—was
the communications room.

The ventilators roared. The ringing walls were like
a trap. The hounds held their heads low, rumbling.

In flight, in null gravity, this well would be the fore-
and-aft axis of the ship. A metal pole, shiny with use,
stretched up the center, affording handholds for men
to pull themselves along in free fall, graceful as dart-
ing fish. Now, in the vertical position, with the solid
pull of a planet underfoot, there were lifts to transport men and supplies to platforms that jutted out beside access hatches at each level.

Stark had no desire to commit himself to one of
those lifts, but he could see no other way. He climbed
onto the nearest one, with Ashton and Pedrallon and
the two hounds. The platform was wide and it had a
rail around it. Gerd and Grith crowded close against
Stark and trembled; and when he pressed the button
on the panel and the platform shot up smoothly on its
steel channels, their minds were filled with the fear of
unknown things and the emptiness that yawned beneath
their feet.

Watch!

We watch, N'Chaka.

The lift went up swiftly, past the lower levels.

N'Chaka! There!

"There" was an access hatch on the opposite side
of the well. It was open. The platform it served was
above the lift, which was rising toward it. It was
below the next platform on the near side of the well,
so that the lift would have to pass it in order for the
occupants to gain access to the top levels. An old
Earth saying flashed across Stark's mind, not a com-

forting one. Something about shooting fish in a barrel.
"I heard," Ashton said.

"Fire!"

They fired together at the opening. Harsh thunder
crashed in the well. The metal surrounding the hatch
became pocked and scarred.

The opening was a black throat swallowing death.
The lift drew level, rose above it. No face appeared
in the hatch. No shots came out of it.

Stark and Ashton stopped firing.

Dead?

No. Run. Think harm later.

Two men, unhurt, armed, were waiting to try again.

Stark punched a red button on the control panel.
The lift came up to the platform and stopped.

Beyond the access hatch, in the crew's quarters,
they found bodies. Two were in a corridor, where
they had tried to run. Three others were inside a small
wardroom, where death had interrupted them at lunch.

Stark located a vertical hatchway with a ladder
fixed to the wall. The hounds would not be able to
climb it, but that seemed to be the only way up.

Where men?

Close!

Stark pulled himself up the ladder.

He emerged on the flight deck. The primary control
banks took up most of the central portion of this level,
with computer linkages and the navigation tank. At
his left, on the far side of the bridge, was the communications center. Two more bodies were huddled
there. One of them had fallen from the radioman's
chair.

N'Chaka! Danger! There!

"There" was behind him.

He dropped, rolling. The first burst went over him.
He heard shattering noises and thought, Oh God, if
they've wrecked the radio . . . !

Ashton had come up the ladder behind Stark. He
fired from the level of the deck. Something blew up
with a tremendous bang. Then Stark was firing from

where he lay, at two figures indistinct in the sudden smoke.

Abruptly it was quiet. The smoke dissipated. The men lay on the deck and Gerd was saying, *Dead.*

Stark got up and went over to the radio.

Ashton climbed the rest of the way up the ladder and joined him. "It's all right? They didn't hit it?"

"They didn't hit it." Stark dragged the radioman's body away from the chair.

Simon Ashton sat down. He switched power into the hyperbeam transmitter and turned on the recorder. He began to send. Pedrallon came in and stood beside him. The Skaithian watched intently, though Ashton was speaking Universal and he could not understand what was said.

Ashton had chosen his words carefully. He kept the message short, accenting the urgency of his request for a rescue ship. He mentioned Penkawr-Che and his reavers. "I am sending from one of their transmitters, which we shall have to abandon. We will try to make radio contact with any incoming ship. Failing that, the ship will please make a landing on the high heath southwest of Skeg and wait there as long as it reasonably can." He used a code signal for "Top Priority," making it mandatory that anyone receiving the message should relay it immediately to Pax. Then he set the switch on AUTOMATIC SEND and left the recorder on at REPEAT. The message would continue to be transmitted until someone came to shut it off.

"That's all we can do," he said. "That, and pray that somebody hears it."

Pedrallon pictured the terrible black emptiness of space, and was not cheered.

Stark fired a sustained burst into the control banks, making a satisfying mess. A disabled ship and a message sent would give the looters something to think about. Penkawr-Che might even abandon his planned foray against the House of the Mother.

He went over and looked at the bodies of the two men who had not "heard" the Northhounds. They did not in any way resemble each other. Stark nudged one of them with his foot.

"He was in the pit by the middle cannon this morning. If he hadn't been relieved . . ."

He turned to Ashton, thinking of the hoppers that must be well on their way back to the ship by now, unless the radioman had died before he could send off a call, and thinking also that there might be more like these two aboard them.

"Ten minutes to search for a portable radio. Then we go."

They found it in five, in a stores room on the level below, where the men apparently outfitted themselves for shoregoing expeditions. They also found arms racks, empty because the weapons were all in use, oxygen packs and protective clothing for climates not quite unfriendly enough to require full-dress armor, and several different types of portable communicators. Stark chose two powerful miniaturized radios in high-impact cases, easily carried and suitable for ground-to-ground or ground-to-orbit use. They also took as much ammunition as they could carry for the automatic weapons.

Going down on the lift, the silent ship was an iron tomb around them. Gerrith touched Stark's arm and smiled, then accompanied him out into the sunshine.

There was still no sound of motors in the sky.

Halk disabled the cannon. He and the Irnanese hurried with Stark and the others across the gravel plain. The dead hounds were gone; Tuchvar had carried them into the jungle for burial. In the fringe of trees beyond the stream the tribesmen stood by their cannon, waiting.

Sabak said longingly, "Can't we take it with us?"

Stark shook his head. "Too heavy, and we're in a hurry."

Somebody hacked the cable. Tuchvar came up with red eyes and his surviving hounds. The line formed, and Larg led the party swiftly away into the jungle.

The journey back to the sea took them longer than the journey inland, because they must needs spend hours motionless under the trees, lest the furiously questing hoppers find them. At length they no longer heard the snarling of motors overhead, and Stark concluded that the search had been dropped in favor of more pressing work, such as repairing the ship or making arrangements to shift their loot to one of the other craft.

Larg went quietly back to his village, and the rest of the party returned to the inlet very late in the second night. The Tarf were on guard, undisturbed. Stark and the others clambered aboard the boat.

The Fallarin, their dark fur patched with sweat, listened to the news, and Alderyk said impatiently, "So, then, it was worth the effort. Now let us be gone from this place. The jungle winds are slow and stupid, and they bring us no comfort."

He spread his wings and gave the sluggish air a spiteful slap.

Under oars, the boat crept out into open water, and when the sail went up the winged men filled it with a whistling breeze.

They headed southward, partly because of Gerrith's vision and partly because there was no other place to go. Northward were only enemies. In the south, Gerrith told them, were help and hope, though the white mists still clung heavily about the shape of them, so that she could not discern them clearly, and in that whiteness there was still the spreading stain of blood.

Stark said, "We'll make for Iubar. The Lady Sanghalain can give us news of the White South, if nothing else."

It was in his mind that the Lady Sanghalain might not be overjoyed to receive him, since it was by his urging that she had taken passage in *Arkeshti* and so the treasure of Iubar had found its way into Penkawr-Che's pocket. Still, it was the only place to start.

So they moved into strange waters, under strange

skies, as foreign to these northern folk of Skaith as to the off-worlders.

They moved as Old Sun moved, with the winter at their backs, toward the austral spring.

But there was no spring.

18

At first they had threatening sails behind them out of
Cereleng, sweeping the sea in search of the lost prince.
Whenever the sails came too close, the Fallarin sent
adverse winds, sudden gusts to split canvas and snap
spars. After a time, they saw no more sails except those
of fishermen; and sometimes, far out on the horizon,
the topsails of a deep-sea trader that seemed to stand
still, like a tiny patch of cloud caught between sea and
sky.

They were seldom out of sight of land. Avoiding
cities, or towns of any size, they ran in to fishing
villages for fresh water and supplies. They had nothing
with which to barter and so were reduced to stealing,
with the aid of the hounds, but they took no more than
was necessary to keep them alive. And the country
was fat, so that a modest theft of fish and fruit wrought
no hardship even on the poor.

But as they went farther down the curve of Mother
Skaith's last green girdle, the Fertile Belt, this richness
began to wither. The air, which had been soft and
indolent, turned sharper. The milky sea grew dark.
Along the shore, plantations of trees that ought to have
been in blossom, or bearing fruit, were blackened by
unprecedented frost. There began to be abandoned
farmsteads beside blasted orchards and cold fields
where seed had died in the ground. Forest as well as
orchard had suffered heavily. They passed miles of
skeletal trees, and where these gave way to scrub hills
and open savannah, they began to come upon plun-

dered villages, often with squattering tracks on the fore-
shore where the Children of the Sea had been. Farther
inland they could see smoke and knew that other
villages were burning.

They were careful where they landed now. Old Sun's
face was hidden more and more behind dark clouds,
and the Northhounds roused and snuffed the wind that
blew against them out of the White South.

Snow, N'Chaka! Snow!

They began to encounter the elements of a vast
army, advancing northward.

Some came by land, entire villages marching with
their women and children, or bands of stragglers
wandering wild along the shore. Others came by sea,
in single sails or in squadrons that dotted the gray
water with bright-painted hulls. All shared one thing
in common.

Hunger.

"My lady Cold has been beforehand here," said
Gerrith. "See how her daughter walks with these folk,
like a faithful sister. The winter has been long, and
it shows no sign of leaving. All their stock is used up
and they are driven north toward the green lands."
She smiled, without joy. "I told you the Goddess would
move this wintertime. I had forgotten that the seasons
are upside down in this underside of Skaith, and she
has been at work through all these long months while
we were lulled by summer."

"The whole south seems to be on the move," said
Stark. "The people of Iubar may be among them."

Gerrith shook her head. "No. This is only the first
wave of the Second Wandering. Iubar has not yet
stirred."

"Well," said Stark, "if they migrate, it will be by
sea and not by land. We can keep watch for them."

"It will not be necessary," Gerrith said.

And it was not.

Meanwhile, by radio, Ashton kept track as well as
he could of Penkawr-Che and his ships.

He heard much talk back and forth between *Arkeshti*

and the other two. The second ship, which had found leaner pickings on its way back from Iubar, joined *Arkeshti* on the heath at about the same time that Stark's party attacked the third ship in Andapell. Stark and Ashton listened to some furious conversations. Ashton's call for help, and his message about Penkawr-Che and his captains, had caused panic in some quarters.

Penkawr-Che held it down. There was no certainty, he said, that the transmission had been picked up, or that it would be forwarded if it had been. And one man's statement was no proof of anything, even if that man *were* Simon Ashton. Assuming the worst, it would still take time for any GU ship to reach Skaith.

It was decided to finish up and get out well before the earliest possible deadline, calculated on the dispatch of a ship from the nearest GU base. But the big problem facing Penkawr-Che was the Andapell ship, which Stark had severely disabled. The owner-skipper insisted on repairs and demanded help.

Prudence dictated abandonment, since repairs would cause more delay than they could reasonably afford. Greed considered the loss of a fat cargo, which could not be easily transshipped because of the logistics involved, and also because there would not be room for it in the two remaining ships unless the attempt to loot the House of the Mother should be dropped. Nobody wanted to drop that, especially not the skipper of the second ship, who felt disadvantaged.

Greed won. From the three ships, technicians and spare parts were mustered to patch up the control system. The third ship finally lifted off and went into a stationary orbit above the heath. *Arkeshti* and the second ship joined it there. Then they shifted orbit together and dropped down over the curve of the world, and Ashton lost them.

The three ships landed on the Plain of Worldheart, under the wall of the Witchfires, where the aurora danced on glittering peaks.

The triple shock of that landing was felt in the deep levels where the Children of Skaith-Our-Mother tended their gardens and fretted at the change of temperature that had lately become apparent. Only a matter of two or three degrees; but in a closed environment, where there had been not the slightest change for centuries, the rich crops seemed suddenly frail and vulnerable.

Word of the shock was carried upward through the maze of carven halls, to the ears of Kell à Marg, Skaith-Daughter. And presently she looked down once again from her high window above the plain.

She saw the hoppers rise and bumble along the mountain wall, a droning swarm of inquisitive bees searching for the doorway to the honeypot.

Kell à Marg set watchers where there had been no need of watchers since the last of the Wandering. She spoke to her captains. Then she went with her chief Diviner through long, dim corridors past monastic quarters where young Diviners were trained—so few of them now, she thought, so very few, with how many deserted chambers on all sides—to the place where the Eye of the Mother was kept, in the great Hall of the Diviners.

The hall was circular, with a high vault from which a lamp of pierced silver depended. The lamp was unlit. Small lamps flickered round the circumference of the walls, which had once been hung with an ancient and holy tapestry known as the Veil, from which the face of the Mother, many times repeated, had looked benignly upon her children. Nothing was left of the Veil now but blackened tatters, and the walls themselves were scorched. This sacrilege had been done by a creature from the Outside, by the sun-haired woman who came with Stark, and both of them prisoners of the Wandsman Gelmar. As always, a small spasm of rage caught at Skaith-Daughter's heart when she looked upon the destruction.

Acolytes brought down the silver lamp on its chain and lighted it. The Diviners gathered round that which was beneath it, a thing waist high and some three feet across, covered with a finely worked cloth.

The cloth was withdrawn, and the Eye of the Mother caught the gleaming of the pierced lamp that swung above. The huge crystal, pellucid as a raindrop, seemed rather to absorb the light than to reflect it, so that the golden rays went glimmering down, and back and forth —now deep, now shallow, ever shifting—and the Diviners bent their heads, gazing with their souls into the depths of the crystal.

Kell à Marg, suppliant, stood waiting.

The Eye of the Mother darkened. The clear shining became curdled and ugly as if it were suffused with blood.

The chief Diviner straightened, sighing. "The end is always the same. And this time is now upon us."

"What comes after it?"

The Diviner bent his head again obediently, though he knew the answer well enough.

Slowly the crystal cleared to the placid blankness of a summer pond.

"Peace," said the Diviner, "though the Mother does not tell us of what sort."

The Eye was covered again, the silver lamp extinguished. Kell à Marg stood in the dim hall, pale-furred, large-eyed, a royal ermine graceful in bands of gold and jewels that made a rich, soft shining even in that half-light. She stood for a long time, and the Diviners stood also.

"If we fled from this place," she said at length, and she was speaking not to the Diviners nor even to herself, but to Someone beyond them all, "what would there be for us in the bitter world? We have given ourselves to the Mother. We cannot go back. Nor can we ever build again as we built here under the Witch-fires. We ourselves are dying. Better to die where we are loved, in the arms of the Mother, than on the cold spears of the wind Outside."

The Diviners sighed, with infinite relief.

"Nevertheless," said Kell à Marg, "if there are those who wish to go, I shall not stop them."

She went from the Hall of the Diviners back to her own place on the knees of the Mother, and she called together her counselors and the Clan-Mothers and the heads of all the guilds—as well as the foremost of the scholars, those who were not too far lost in the vast labyrinthine House that contained the history of a planet, where generations of scholars had studied and catalogued and recreated, deciphering ancient literatures, surmising ancient musics, enjoying learning for its pure and only sake, their minds free, their bodies safe from want.

Surely, thought Kell à Marg, there is no place under the sky for such as these.

She spoke to her people, naming the choices.

"I, myself, will stay," she said, "with those who wish to join me in defending the Mother's House from these off-worlders. Those who wish to face the future elsewhere are free to go by the western gate and the pass that leads to Thyra."

No one chose to leave.

Kell à Marg rose. "Good. We shall die well—now, if we must, by the hand of the invader, or later, by the hand of time. In either case, we remain true to ourselves and to the choice we made long ago. It would not become us to outlive the Mother."

She turned to her chamberlain. "There is armor somewhere, I believe. Find it."

The Children of Skaith-Our-Mother made ready.

The attack did not come.

The hoppers bumbled up and down along the mountain wall, searching. The high windows of the Mother's House were not easily distinguished among the million rough, ice-coated crevices of the rock. The hoppers were plagued by winds, and by blizzards that hid the Witchfires in blinding snow. The Children began to hope that the off-worlders would go away.

They stayed.

Twice, hoppers swept in over the pass and battered

the blank stone under the Leaning Man, and the Children slid the great blocks of their inner defenses into place. The second time, explosive charges burst in the outer gate. The Leaning Man fell down and sealed the opening with more tons of shattered rock than the offworlders cared to move. They returned to the plain and continued their stubborn search. Though Kell à Marg could not know it, their time was growing very short.

In the end, it was the carelessness, or the overeagerness, of a watcher that betrayed the Children: he allowed himself to be seen on one of the balconies, and the invasion began.

The winds were calm that day, with Old Sun blinking a dim eye above the peaks. The craft were able to maneuver close to the cliffs. Lightning bolts struck through the opening, licking along the corridor within. The watcher had given warning, and the Children were not there, so that the laser beams struck only unoffending rock.

After the laser beams came men. They entered the House of the Mother.

The invaders entered into darkness, for the Children had taken away the lamps; but they brought lights of their own, harsh white beams that slashed the blackness without really illuminating it. They took up positions in the corridor, with automatic weapons at the ready, covering the arrival of more men, winched down on swaying cables like the first.

The corridors and lightless chambers all around remained silent. The air smelled of dust and sweet oil and something else the off-worlders could not quite define—time, perhaps, or the subtle breath of decay exhaled from the millions of stored, separate things gathered in the uncounted rooms cut from the heart of the mountain.

They heard sounds. Whisperings. Breathings. Soft, hurried footfalls. But the stone vaults distorted sound so that they could not be sure whether what they heard was the echoes of their own movements, or something more sinister.

They found the weight of their heavy weapons comforting, knowing that there was nothing in these catacombs that could stand against them.

The Children knew that, too.

"Wait," said Kell à Marg in her beautiful, useless armor. "If they believe that we will not attack them, they may become careless."

"But they have already begun to plunder our treasures," said one of the younger captains. "Is it not our place to die well, defending them?"

"There is always time for that," said Kell à Marg, "and opportunity will not be lacking. Meantime, prepare more poisoned shafts for the crossbows."

The Children had not been forced to fight since the turbulent days of the Wandering, and that was long ago. They were not skilled with weapons, and their swords were wrought more for beauty than for use. The small, light crossbows they carried were not built to throw their bolts for long distances, because in these catacombs all distances were short; and they had little power of penetration. But once dipped in the paste made from a certain fungus grown in the lower levels, the slender bolts did not need to penetrate. A scratch was sufficient.

The Children, with their flitting lamps, kept out of sight of the intruders, moving in side corridors and through the maze of adjacent rooms. When the captains came, they knew it. When the men, growing bolder as nothing appeared to threaten them, spread out through the rock-cut chambers, the Children knew that, too, spying secretly from carved doorways.

The invaders were choosy. They wanted small things, easily portable: statuary, jewelry, fine weapons, paintings, books, any objects sufficiently alien and strange to attract connoisseurs of the *outré*. They became engrossed in their search, pawing among large and heavy things for the little pearls. Load after load went to the hoppers. Men began to pick up what they could to hide on their persons. The weather held calm, and each room led to another, and still another.

Suddenly, in one of the high windows above the plain, a watcher saw black clouds blot out the Bleak Mountains with trailing skirts of snow. He sent word to Kell à Marg.

The invaders got the same news, and began to move toward the hoppers, which would soon be forced to land and wait out the blizzard. Strung out in twos and threes among the treasure rooms, the men grabbed what they could carry.

The Children struck.

They struck from dark chambers as the bright lights left. They struck from shadowy doorways. The invaders were professionals; they retreated in good order. But the Children were ahead of them and all around them. The aliens caught glimpses of white-furred bodies in glittering mail. They saw the mad eyes of night-dwelling creatures glowing at them, swiftly vanishing in the all-encompassing labyrinth. They heard the click and whir of the crossbows, such feeble little things against the bursts of their automatics that filled the stony spaces with chattering thunder. The automatics killed; they killed quite a number of the Children. But there were always more, and their little sharp bolts went whispering into flesh and it mattered not how quickly they were withdrawn.

The star-captains and the last of their remaining crews were hauled up into the hoppers.

After the sound of the rotors had died away, Kell à Marg and her captains, such as were left of them, came out into the main corridor. She looked at the scattered loot, and the scattered bodies.

"Let the bodies of the off-worlders be cast from the balcony, and let those things which are ours be replaced. Then give orders to the Guild of Masons. Every window that looks upon the world is to be blocked up forever. The gates are already sealed. We will use whatever time is left us to further our knowledge and leave what records we may of the life-tale of Mother Skaith, here in her eternal House."

It mattered not to Kell à Marg, nor to any of the Children, that those reports would never be read.

Those whose duty it was lifted the fallen Children and bore them down through the labyrinth to the Hall of Joyful Rest, where they were united with the Mother.

Skaith-Daughter returned to her place upon the knees of the Mother. She leaned her head back, into the polished hollow between the Mother's breasts. She thought of the off-worlders and the ships and the rending of the barriers that had made this unique and holy planet only one of millions of planets, common as grains of dust across the galaxy. She was sorry that she had lived to see this. She was sorry that, in search of knowledge, she had brought the strangers into the House. She was sorry that she had not killed the man Stark. She hoped that he was dead, or soon would be.

Her tiring-women removed her armor and smoothed her fur with golden combs. She could not hear the picks and hammers of the masons at work, but she knew that in a short time the last of the hateful Outside would be walled away forever. She felt all around her the great, warm, protecting House, the unchanging womb. She set her hands on the hands of Skaith-Mother, and smiled.

In the bitter winds below the pass, where the huge ruin-mound of Thyra bulked, the hearths were cold and no smoke rose from the forges. The Ironmaster and his folk, clanking in their iron gear, burdened with beasts and impedimenta, marched southward under the sign of Strayer's Hammer.

Some days ahead of them, the People of the Towers marched behind the Corn-King and his priests, down across the Darklands.

Southward of both nations, in the Barrens, the Sea of Skorva froze six weeks before its normal time, and the people of Izvand looked with dismay at the drying and salting sheds, which ought to have been filled with

the autumn's heavy catch, and which were empty.
Izvand supplied mercenaries for the Wandsmen; and
now the wolf-eyed fighting men began, in their turn,
to wonder about the winter that lay ahead, thinking of
fatter fields they knew below the Border, in the Fertile
Belt.

In the high passes of the mountains, early snows
caught traders and travelers by surprise. Herdsmen
moved their flocks from summer pastures struck by
freezing rains. In the rich valleys of the city-states,
harvests withered before blackening frost, and the tithe-
gatherers of the Wandsmen found scant tribute.

In the cold deserts northeast of the Bleak Mountains, at the Place of Winds, the Fallarin listened to
the voices of the high air, which brought them word of
the world, and they took urgent counsel among themselves.

South along the Wandsmen's road, the fortress city
of Yurunna crouched on its rock above the oasis. The
women of the Six Lesser Hearths of Kheb, whose duty
it was to tend the fields, saved what they could while
the irrigation ditches sheeted over with ice and roots
froze in the ground. The men, whose business was war,
turned their veiled faces toward Ged Darod.

And at Ged Darod, the annual tide of Farers flowed
in along the many roads that crossed the plain. They
filled the streets of the city. They filled the squares
and the pleasure gardens. They filled the hostels, and
they ate the food that was always forthcoming from
the Wandsmen's bounty. And still more of them came,
too early and too many, while behind them in the
temperate zone the harvests failed.

The million bells of Ged Darod made joyful music
in a breeze that was not as warm as it might have been.
In the Palace of the Twelve, Ferdias listened to reports
that were in no way joyful, and the first small worm
of doubt crept in behind his triumphant serenity.

19

Below the Fertile Belt, it had become more difficult to evade the bands of refugees who plundered wherever they could in the hope of finding food. Stark steered away, out of sight of land, venturing in only when water became a pressing need.

Upon the sea, food was no longer a problem. Everything was moving north. Aquatic creatures followed shoals of the lesser creatures they fed upon. Winged things, fierce-eyed and whistling, swooped over the surface. Dark, bobbing heads showed where whole colonies of the Children of the Sea-Our-Mother migrated, feeding as they went. The hounds watched constantly, even when they slept, and the men's hands were never far from their weapons.

The boat was under oars much of the time, beating against southerly winds that the Fallarin had not yet learned to tame, though they spent hours in the forepeak with their wings spread, listening, talking.

"They're different from our desert winds," Alderyk said. "They speak of bergs and sea-ice, and they smell of water instead of dust. They have had no one to talk to, and they're proud and wild. They do not learn easily."

Snow came in whirling flakes, and the Northhounds snapped at it like puppies, rolling in the delicious chill where it collected on the deck. The first outriders of the southern ice slipped by, floating mountains glittering and silent amid flat, white pans of drift that thickened imperceptibly across the solemn ocean.

The winds died, through no effort of the Fallarin. Ahead now was a spreading whiteness that swallowed sea and sky together.

Gerrith looked at it and said, "That is where our road leads."

Stark felt the breath of the Goddess upon his cheek and shivered. "She has taken the south for her domain."

"Someone else is there. A woman with strange eyes, who waits for us."

"Sanghalain."

Gerrith repeated, "Sanghalain." And the name sounded like a call to some secret, deadly battle.

The Fallarin found wind enough to fill the sail, but they lacked vigor. Frost clung in their dark fur and rimed the stiff ridges of their wings. It was a chill that nothing could keep out. Men and women huddled together beneath their cloaks, around the galley fire, and Pedrallon shuddered constantly in his blankets. Ashton kept his small radio inside his shirt, lest his fingers freeze to it when he monitored the unchanging silence from the sky. Only the Northhounds throve.

The boat passed into that waiting whiteness. Tendrils of snow-fog wrapped it. It swam englobed in blind mist, with the pan ice rattling and racking along its sides. The men stood at battle stations with their weapons ready, and they saw nothing. The hounds bristled and growled, and gave no warning. Stark held the steering oar, seeing nothing ahead, and behind him the wake vanished as quickly as it was made. He was inured to cold and did not suffer as the others did. But the primitive N'Chaka growled and whimpered within him, as uneasy as the hounds.

Ice finally closed about the boat on all sides and held it fast. Men and hounds stood silent in the silent fog and listened to ghostly voices, the squeaking and grinding and muttering of the floes.

Then another voice spoke in Stark's mind, a deep groaning like a winter tide among rocks.

*I am Morn, Dark Man. You are in my waters. My
army is beneath your keel.*

We come in peace, said Stark.

*Then bid those beasts with the black and burning
minds be still whilst I come aboard.*

They will be still.

Stark spoke to the hounds, and they were shamed
because they had not been aware of Morn and his
people.

Minds shut, N'Chaka. We cannot hear.

Trust them.

Friends?

No. But not enemies.

Not like. Cannot hear.

Trust them.

The hounds' eyes glowed yellow and their tiger claws
scored the deck. But they crouched and were still.

Astern of the boat—where there was open water in
perilous cracks between ice pans—round, shining, hairless heads appeared, heads with great eyes used to
seeing in the ocean depths. And presently Morn hauled
himself huge and dripping over the rail and stood looking at Stark and the hounds, at the Fallarin wrapped in
their dark wings and the Irnanese in their leather and
the tribesmen in their faded cloaks, and at the Tarf,
who regarded him with mild indifference from under
horny lids.

He looked at Gerrith and bent his head briefly.

*Yours is the far-seeing mind. The Lady Sanghalain
has awaited your coming.*

Gerrith bent her head in acknowledgment, but if she
made any answer it was made in mind-talk and Stark
could not hear it. They could all hear Morn when he
wished it, and he could hear them, but the nontelepaths
were deaf to each other except in normal speech.

When Stark had first seen Morn—that time when
Morn and the Lady Sanghalain saved him from the
mob in the pleasure gardens at Ged Darod—Morn had
been clad in ceremonial landgoing gear, a fine garment
of worked and polished leather, and he had carried his

badge of office, a massive trident set with pearls. Now he wore sea-harness, a scant webbing that served only to hold his weapons.

He did not need a badge of office to make him impressive. He stood a head taller than Stark, a natural amphibian evolved from some mammalian ancestor, in contrast to the deliberately mutated Children of the Sea. Unlike the Children, Morn's people were not furred, but had smooth skin, dark on the back and light on the belly, camouflage against deep-swimming predators. Also, they were intelligent and highly organized, with a complex social order of their own. The Children of the Sea hunted them for food, and they hunted the Children of the Sea as vicious brutes, despising them.

Morn's people were called Ssussminh, a name that sounded like rolling surf when it was properly pronounced. They were telepaths because mind-talk was easier than mouth-talk in their watery world; and they had an ancient, mystic, and very powerful connection with the ruling house of Iubar—a connection Stark was sure he would never completely understand. Probably it had begun as a symbiotic partnership, with the Iubarians, who had always been fisher-folk and traders, providing land-based goods and services in exchange for pearls and sea-ivory and such other unique offerings as the Ssussminh might make. Now both members of this ancient partnership were being forced from their homeland by the Dark Goddess.

In any case, Morn was the Lady Sanghalain's other voice. And when he spoke, he spoke to all of them.

At Iubar we are in a trap. Will you enter it? Or will you turn back?

"We cannot turn back," said Gerrith.

Then let us have lines. My people will take you through the pack.

Lines were paid out. The Ssussminh grasped them, many strong swimmers. They towed the boat astern and then ahead again, finding narrow leads which were hidden from a steersman by the fog.

Let your hellhounds watch, douse your fire, and let you all be silent. We must pass through an army.

"Whose?" Stark spoke aloud so that his comrades could follow his end of the conversation. They could all hear Morn.

The Kings of the White Islands have come north, all four tribes, with their belongings and their hunting packs and their sacred island. They besiege Iubar, in force.

"Why?"

The Goddess has told them that it is time for them to go and claim their ancient lands beyond the sea. They need our ships.

"What is their strength?"

Four thousand, more or less, and all fighters, except for those still in the cradle-skins. The women are as fierce as the men, and even the children fight well. Their small javelins fly for the throat.

The boat glided on black water between tumbled plains of ice. Great bergs embedded in the pack showed cliffs and caves where the mist moved vagrant about them, thinning now and then but never lifting. The Ssussminh swam tirelessly. The company stood to arms, making no sound. The hounds watched.

Men, N'Chaka. Men and things, there.

"There" was somewhere ahead.

The bowmen warmed their bows against their bodies, for the cold made them brittle. The strings were inside their shirts to keep them dry. Stark let them stand to, in case they were needed, but he and Simon took the automatics from their place of safety and loaded them. Ammunition was irreplaceable, but this was no time for parsimony. They took up positions on either side of the boat. Morn took the steering oar.

They began to hear voices in the mist, and saw lights, the faint glimmerings of blubber stoves. These were at first before, and then beside, and then behind and all around the boat, which moved with no sound but a gentle purling, creeping through the heart of an army.

N'Chaka! Things come!

The Ssussminh splashed and were gone. The lines fell slack.

The hunting packs have found us. Let your hounds kill now. And let the Fallarin give us way. Hurry!

Alderyk cracked the air with his wings. His fellows joined him. In a moment the sail filled and the boat was moving. The fighting men made ready. In the forepeak, the eyes of the Northhounds brightened and their jaws hung open, panting white smoke.

There came a boiling and moiling in the water. Beasts, shaped like giant otters and furred like snow-leopards, shot up screaming and rolled over to float like dead fish. Then voices shouted alarms off in the fog. Conchs boomed and brayed. Shadows moved on either side, where folk came running in the freezing mist. They ran faster than the boat could swim. Bone-barbed throwing spears rattled inboard.

Stark raised his hand and brought it sharply down. "Now!"

The automatics made bursts of stuttering thunder. Fur-clad forms skittered and fell across the ice. A sort of insane howling rose, and then dropped behind as the boat picked up speed and slid out into open water, leaving the floes astern.

Some trick of the currents, which ran swiftly here along the coast, kept this stretch of water clear of all but broken ice. A fleet of skin boats darted out like beetles from the edges of the floes.

Kill, said Stark, still holding the automatic in case of need.

The hounds growled.

The folk in the boats faltered and lost the paddle stroke, but few of them died, and those not quickly.

Minds fight fear. Strong. Not easy, like most.

Morn said, *The White Islanders are without fear. They are madmen. They have broken themselves by the hundreds against our walls. Now they wait, knowing that we starve. Look there.*

Iubar took form, a dim peninsula ridge-backed with

mountains, snow-covered from the peaks to the sea's edge.

Those fields, said Morn, *should be green, and all this sea clear of ice. But the Goddess holds us fast, pens our ships in the harbor. Even if we could somehow free our ships and try to pass through the floes as we have just done with you, the Islanders would overwhelm us, taking each craft as it came.* He pointed. *There is your anchorage.*

Stark made out a walled town and a harbor. A gray guardian castle bestrode the walls, mailed from its foot with the ice of frozen spray. The single high tower, rising sheer from the rock, bore no battlements. There was no need for defenses atop that unscalable height.

Offshore from the castle, an island reared frosty cliffs above the water. Yet they had not quite the look of cliffs.

Shallafonh, said Morn. *Our city. Looted, like Iubar, and soon to die . . . like Iubar.*

The castle held one side of the harbor mouth in its arm, with a frowning tower for a fist. A second tower faced it across the gap, at the end of a fortified mole. Both towers were armed and manned, and a boom could be drawn to close the narrow entrance. The still water within was choked with ice, but a way had been cleared for Stark's boat to the end of the royal quay.

Let be, said Morn to the Fallarin, and they were glad to stop because the Goddess sapped their strength. Some of Morn's people caught the trailing lines again. The boat was brought into harbor, with film ice already forming behind it, and was moored beside what Stark was sure must be Sanghalain's own ship. Everywhere at the quays, white-shrouded ships lay motionless and all the normal voices of the harbor were mute.

And so, said Morn, *you are safely within the trap, though for what reason I do not yet know.*

Stark looked toward Gerrith, but she had gone apart from them.

The sail folded down like a tired wing. Men and

women sat stiffly, unable to comprehend that they had reached the end of the voyage.

The great portal of the castle tower opened. A woman clad in brown appeared, and Stark knew that it must be Sanghalain and that there were people with her. But he could only watch Gerrith.

A change had come over her. She seemed to have grown taller, to have shed all the weariness and uncertainty of the voyage. She walked to the gunwale and mounted it and stepped onto the quay, and no one dreamed of offering her a hand. Stark moved to follow her, and then stopped. On the tower steps, Sanghalain and her ladies and her courtiers stood still.

Gerrith looked about her, at the shrouding mist and the dead sky. A sort of glory seemed to touch her. She shook back the hood that covered her head and her hair shone with its own light. Sun-colored woman, shining in this place of death. And Stark's heart turned in him like a sword blade.

Gerrith spoke, and her voice rang like a sweet, strong bell against the bitter stones.

"I know now why my way has led me to this place."

Sanghalain came down the steps. The courtiers remained where they were, but a double file of women followed her, all in habits of brown wool, all with faces hidden behind brown veils. They marched along the quay and halted before Gerrith, who had turned to meet them. All the brown habits bent and swayed in a kind of genuflection. Sanghalain stretched out her hands.

Gerrith took them. The two women looked at each other, motionless, their hands clasped together. Then they turned, and the file turned with them, somber skirts whipping in the wind, moving back toward the steps.

And once again Stark stood, in memory, in the House of the Ironmaster at Thyra, when Hargoth the Corn-King turned in his rage upon Gerrith, whom he himself had wished to sacrifice. "You prophesied for me, Sun Woman," he had said. "Now I prophesy for you. Your body will yet feed Old Sun, though not as a parting gift."

Stark sprang onto the quay. He started after Gerrith, and Morn stood before him.

She goes of her own free will, Dark Man.

"For a sacrifice? Is that why Sanghalain was waiting for her?"

The hounds were beside Stark now. But others of the Ssussminh had gathered, barring his way. They were armed, and the hounds were of no use against them. Stark saw archers in Sanghalain's livery standing with ready bows on the lower defenses of the castle.

We will slay you all, if we must, Morn said. *It will not change this matter.*

Gerrith walked with the Lady of Iubar, up the steps and into the cold, gray tower.

20

They were in a cold stone room with faded tapestries on the walls and a tiny fire of sea-coals on the hearth. Sanghalain and the brown-veiled women of the Sisterhood of which she was High Priestess had been with Gerrith all night. They had withdrawn now, so that the wise woman of Irnan might have time alone with her companions.

She was clothed in a gown the color of her hair, which hung loose over her shoulders, glowing brighter than the firelight. She sat at a table, her head bent above a basin filled with pellucid water, provided for her by the Sisterhood.

Halk, Alderyk, Pedrallon, and Sabak stood near the table, waiting for her to speak. Simon Ashton stood by himself, a little way apart. Stark remained at the far end of the room, as distant from Gerrith as he could be, looking as if he might kill her himself if she were within his reach.

When she spoke, with the voice of the prophetess, he listened as the others did. But there was that in his face that made Ashton glance at him uneasily.

"The folk of the north have begun their Second Wandering," she said. "The Fallarin have abandoned the Place of Winds."

The sudden clap of Alderyk's wings made the candles gutter.

"They go south to Yurunna," she continued, "and such as are left of the Ochar move that way also. At Yurunna, many of the tribesmen make ready to move, for they have not enough from the ruined crops to carry them through the winter."

Sabak's blue eyes were intense above the tribal veil.

Gerrith went on. "Across the Bleak Mountains, the Witchfires are sealed. Skaith-Daughter and her people have made their choice. Penkawr-Che's ships—and I think they got little from the Children for their pains —have left the planet. The Harsenyi were scattered long since, down the southern roads.

"The forges of Thyra are cold and the people march. Hargoth the Corn-King leads his narrow folk south from the Towers. At Izvand, the wolf-eyed men look toward the Border. Other folk, whose names I do not know, are leaving their starving places. There will be much fighting, but the city-states will hold behind their walls. Irnan alone will be abandoned, for lack of food, and I see smoke above the rooftops. Her people will find refuge among the other city-states."

Halk bit his lip, but did not speak.

"The southern wave of the wandering will die out as the survivors find better lands. Pedrallon's country and others like it can absorb most of the refugees, though their way of life will be greatly changed. But there is no help there for our cause. It is from here, from the White South, as I foretold, that our armies will come. Sanghalain, by her arts, knows that there is no longer any place on Skaith for her people or for the Ssussminh. Their only hope lies in the star-ships."

Stark spoke abruptly, and his words were like daggers. "I will not serve Sanghalain."

"There is no need to. When that has happened which will happen, make alliance with the Kings of the White Islands. They will be your spearhead. You shall lead them."

"Why?"

She recognized the twofold nature of his question.

"Because you are the Dark Man of the prophecy, fated whether you will or no, and the threads of your fate are knotted together in one place—Ged Darod, where you will fight your last battle with Ferdias and the Wandsmen. A battle you must win." She held up her hand to stop him speaking. "You care nothing for the prophecy, I know. You came here for one purpose, to rescue Simon Ashton. The ship you called for will come, but the Lords Protector now have the power to interfere with it. The off-world thing that Pedrallon left behind is in their hands."

"The transceiver," Pedrallon said.

Gerrith nodded. "You must make haste with your army, Stark. If you do not, the Lords Protector will send the ship away, or destroy it, and there will be no escape for you, forever."

"We also have transceivers," Ashton reminded her.

She shook her head. "I see you marching mute to Ged Darod, with nothing of the off-worlds in your hands."

"Not even the automatics?"

"Not even those."

Ashton glanced at Stark, but his eyes were on Gerrith, seeing nothing else.

"Will the Kings of the White Islands fight?" asked Halk. "Why should they help us?"

"Because they wish to regain their ancient lands."

"And where are these lands?"

"Where Ged Darod now stands."

A long silence followed. Gerrith continued to look into the clear water. Then she sighed and leaned back. "I see no more." She looked at them, smiling gravely. "You have been good comrades. We have fought well together. You will see to the end of that fighting. Go now, and remember that the respite will be a short one. The Goddess has set her hand on Iubar."

They bent their heads, all but Alderyk, who gave her a king's salute. They left, and Simon Ashton went with them.

Stark remained.

He went no closer to Gerrith, as though he did not trust himself. "Will nothing turn you aside from this obscenity?" he said, and his voice was a cry of pain.

Gerrith looked at him with love, with tenderness.

She looked at him from faraway, from some place he did not know and could not enter, but which he hated with every fiber of his being.

"This is my destiny," she said gently. "My duty, my high honor. This was the thing I had yet to do, so that I could not go with the others on the starship. This was why my path led me southward into the white mist, though I could see nothing there but blood. *My* blood, I know now."

"And Sanghalain will hold the knife?"

"That is her task. Through the sacrifice of my body to Old Sun, many lives will be saved, and my world set free. Do not betray me, Stark. Do not let what I do be wasted because of your anger. Lead, as you were fated to lead, for my sake."

Little flames hissed among the coals. Sleet tapped against the windowpanes. Stark could bear her gaze no longer. He bent his head and Gerrith smiled with a remote tenderness.

"Remember all the long way we had together and be glad for it, as I am."

Stark's heart was frozen in him and he could not speak. He turned and left her, walking softly, as one leaves a house of death.

In the drafty hall Sanghalain waited, with her veiled women robed all in brown, and her honor guard, and Morn. The Lady of Iubar wore the same brown habit. Her body was full and gracious, a very woman's body, small in the waist, rounded of breast and hip. Her hair was black, one shining loop of it showing above her forehead where her veil was thrown back. She wore no jewels—all those were now in Penkawr-Che's coffers—and her face showed the pinched lines of care. Her eyes were like the winter sea where the sun strikes it, gray with depths and darknesses and sudden tides of light. Eyes in which, Stark had felt, a man might lose himself and drown. Once he had thought her beautiful. Now, as he moved closer to her, Morn set his hand upon his knife.

Sanghalain met Stark's gaze calmly and without concern. "This is our world," she said. "You have no part in it, nor in its customs."

"That is true," said Stark. "Nevertheless, do not let me look upon you again."

He went away, along the cold corridor.

Sanghalain and her brown-veiled women entered Gerrith's room.

"It is time," said Sanghalain.

And Gerrith answered, "I am ready."

She walked with the Lady of Iubar and her women through the echoing ways of the tower. Morn and the honor guard followed with torches. A winding stair led upward to the tower top. They mounted it and came out upon the wide, flat, icy stones that stretched away to the sheer edges and the drop beyond. In the center of the round space a kind of bier had been erected and draped with rich fabrics to hide the faggots of wood piled beneath. It was still dark. The dead-white mist of the Goddess enfolded the tower, so that the torches burned only feebly.

Gerrith stood silent, facing the east.

At length, in the dark and the frost-fog, low on the horizon there crept a faint smudge of coppery light.

Sanghalain held out her hand to Morn. "The knife."

He gave it to her, across his two hands, bowing low. The women began to chant, very softly. Sanghalain veiled her face.

Gerrith walked to the bier, a sacrifice going proudly, consenting.

She lay down, and saw the knife blade shining above her in the white air, striking swiftly downward.

When Old Sun rose, a dull ghost behind the shrouding mist, the folk of the White Islands saw a great blaze of flame on the tower top, and wondered.

Eric John Stark went alone with his grief and anger into the barren hills, and no one—not even Simon Ashton—tried to find him. But the Northhounds howled without ceasing for three days, a terrible requiem for the wise woman of Irnan.

21

The hellish part of the ritual was that it worked.

After that burst of flame on the tower top, the mist began almost imperceptibly to thin. At noon, the face of Old Sun was clearly seen for the first time in un-remembered months, and folk ran out to stand in the snow and feel his touch upon them. Then a wind blew warm from the north. By that afternoon the thaw had begun.

It continued. As torrents rushed down the slopes and the ice began to go from the harbor, the people of Iubar, reborn, revitalized, flung themselves into the task of clearing and refitting their ships.

The people of the White Islands, with their floes be-ginning to rot away beneath them, attacked Iubar in successive waves of desperation. But the boom had closed the harbor mouth to boats, and the land walls held.

On the fourth day, Stark came back from his wander-ing, gaunt and strange-eyed. He would not enter the tower. He went directly to the boat and sent a mes-senger to bring his people.

They came, and no one ventured to speak to him except Halk, who faced him squarely and said, "She had a better death than Breca."

Stark inclined his head and turned away to speak to Ashton.

"Have you heard anything on the radio?"

"Nothing yet."

Stark nodded. "You'd better wait here, Simon. I'm

going to parley with the Kings, and they may not give us a chance to talk."

Simon shrugged and sat down in his accustomed place, taking charge of the two automatics.

Stark ordered the oars out. But at the last minute, Morn came padding down the quay.

I will go with you, Dark Man.

Stark looked at him with utter hatred. "Why?"

Because you do not know the Kings, you do not even know their names. You know nothing of their customs or their history. You will never arrange a parley without me.

Stark hesitated, then nodded curtly. Morn stepped aboard. The Northhounds growled, and Stark bade them be quiet. The rowers dipped their blades in the water and the boat moved out toward the harbor mouth, where the boom was swung aside enough to let them through.

While they rowed across the open water, Morn talked. And because Simon Ashton had taught him well, Stark listened.

When the first of the skin boats came out to challenge them, Stark shouted, "We claim the Peace of Gengan and the Holy Isle of Kings! Who denies us this is cursed."

Reluctantly the people in the skin boats put their weapons aside and formed into a sort of ragged escort, while four of the boats darted off among the rotting, jostling floes.

Stark could see that numbers of the White Islanders had been forced to move their skin tents onto the shore, wherever they could find high ground. The people in the boats had stripped their outer furs in the glow of the ginger star, which had been bought at such price, and their heads were bare. They seemed to run to every shade of color in their hair, which was clubbed, warrior-fashion, to give no grip to a foe. Their faces were uniformly windburned, a paler streak rimming each face where the tight fur hoods normally covered them. Their faces were also uniformly savage, with powerful jaws and cheek ridges, and deep-sunk eyes that carried an expression of single-minded ferocity. Stark wondered if these people would ever be found relaxed and smiling.

One of the skin boats took the lead, and Stark steered after it until they reached a solid line of ice so old and thick that it had barely begun to wear away in the sunlight.

The rest of the journey must be done on foot, said Morn. *See there.*

Stark saw the crest of a giant berg glittering in the sun.

That is the Holy Isle. Leave your hounds and your weapons. You will have no need of them. Bring an escort, but no more than four besides ourselves.

Ashton came, and Alderyk, and Halk, and Pedrallon. Sabak was left in charge of the boat, Tuchvar of the hounds. He had difficulty controlling them. The smell of violence and the red thought of killing were all around.

The Islanders hauled their skin boats onto the ice and followed. Afoot, they moved with a kind of controlled ferocity, setting their feet as a hunting animal does before the spring. But their weapons remained untouched.

They are fighters, Morn said, catching Stark's thought. *Killing machines. They are bred to nothing else. Any child that shows fear or weakness is thrown to the hunting packs.*

Some of the leopard-spotted beasts had come onto the ice, moving agilely enough on their short powerful legs, with broad paws that could disembowel a man in one swift stroke. The Islanders kept an eye on them, and from time to time beat back those which became too much interested in the foreign-smelling flesh.

The shining peak of the berg came closer. Stark could see its foot, broad and massive, a veritable island of ice. The clear slopes rose above, and they were marked with curious dark blots, set in regular ranks one above the other.

Morn said, *That is where they bury their kings.*

Four men stood before a standard set on a high pole of sea-ivory cunningly joined and bound. The standard flashed in the sun with the untarnished brilliance that only gold can show. Its top was in the shape of a man's head, somewhat larger than life, and the expression of the face was one of gentle and sorrowful dignity.

Beneath it the four Kings of the White Islands regarded the foreigners with the eyes of wolverines.

Delbane and Darik, Astrane and Aud, the Sons of Gengan.

Four separate small knots of people stood near the Kings, presumably their honor guards. And all up and down and across the slopes of the berg, the dead kings watched, upright in their burial niches, sealed in the ice and preserved without change by the perpetual cold. Stark could not count them, and presumably the ranks extended around the berg where he could not see.

Trickles of water were beginning to run down those cliffs, and Stark wondered what would happen to the Holy Isle as the tribes moved northward.

They will leave it here, said Morn, *under the care of the Goddess. They will take with them only the Head of Gengan.*

A herald came forward. He was dressed no differently from the other Islanders, but he carried a staff of sea-ivory topped with a small copy of the Head, which was also wrought in gold.

"Who are you, who would speak with the Four Kings? This one we know, his people are our old enemies." He gestured with his staff at Morn. "But you are strangers. You came from the north, with his help, and killed many of our people with unknown weapons. Why should the Four Kings grant you audience?"

"Because," said Stark, "they wish to regain the lands from which their forefathers were driven. We can help them."

The herald returned to the standard. He spoke with the Kings. Then he marched back.

"Come," he said. And when they had advanced, he said, "Stand here."

The four killer faces fronted them, under circlets of ivory set with great pearls brought out of the sea. The glance of their small, bright eyes was a stabbing rather than a seeing. Like their people, they had had all the softer places of the soul cut ruthlessly away, leaving nothing of love or laughter or mercy or kindness. The hairs rose at the back of Stark's neck, and N'Chaka repressed a challenging snarl.

The four pairs of eyes roved over Ashton; over Alderyk, pausing curiously; over Pedrallon, hunched in his furs; over Halk's tall bulk. They settled at last on Stark, and stayed there. Something in his dark face and cold, light eyes spoke to them.

"We march northward to the sun," said Delbane, the oldest of the Kings, and Stark recognized something in the man that he had seen before in the High North: the madness of a too-long prisoning in cold and darkness. "We have waited for generations, preparing ourselves. Now the Goddess has told us it is time. We are fated. How can such as you give us help?"

"You have lost the ships of Iubar," Stark said, and the warmth of Old Sun on his face was like the warmth of shed blood. "Your people must do their marching on land, at least for the time being, since your skin boats won't live in the open sea. You know nothing of the world, and the north is full of hostile people. If you march alone, you will never see those lands you covet."

Aud, the youngest of the Kings, leaped forward as though to sink his powerful teeth in Stark's throat. Instead, he began to orate, stamping his feet and flinging his arms wide.

"For generations! You heard him say it, my brother-enemy. Countless years of waiting, until we were ready. You see there, the golden head? That is the head of Gengan, who was our lord and king at the time of the Wandering. He was a philosopher, a peaceable man. We were a peaceable people, we bore no arms, we kept no army, we were proud of our pious and lofty peacefulness.

"But when the strong hands of well-armed countries, under which we had sheltered, let go, and the wolves they had held in check were loosed upon us with their weapons, we could do nothing but run.

"We ran, all down the curve of Mother Skaith. And at last, the remnant of us were driven far into the White South, into a place so cruel and barren that no one else wanted it; and there we halted, and survived.

"We taught ourselves new skills. The four grandsons of Gengan became each one a king over a fourth of our people, and each fourth has been at perpetual war with the other three. Only the fierce and the able live, and if they live too long they are sent to the Goddess. Now we are ready. Now we go to take back what was ours, to live again under the sun."

Aud ceased his orating and looked contemptuously at the strangers. "If a child cries in the cold we slay it, so that weak seed will not be passed on. How can soft creatures like you be of use to us?"

"These soft creatures managed to kill quite a number of your people," said Stark, showing the edges of his teeth.

A dull flush came across Aud's cheekbones and his eyes burned. Stark stepped past him and spoke to the elder Kings.

"Do you know where to find your lost lands?"

Each King drew from among his furs a golden plaque, pierced at the top to hang about the neck on a leather cord. Each plaque showed an identical map, deeply incised; and though the scale was all wrong, Stark was able to recognize the general contours of sea and land, the place where Skeg now stood, and the plain of Ged Darod to the northeast.

He placed a finger on Delbane's plaque. "Here," he said, and they were astonished, catching their breath sharply.

"How can you know?" demanded Aud. "You, a stranger?"

"Strangers often possess some scraps of knowledge. For instance, I can tell you that a great and powerful city stands there, the city of the Wandsmen, which you will be forced to take before you can occupy your land again."

He turned and swept his hand in a wide gesture across the floes. "You are fighters and know no fear. But you could not break the walls of Iubar. Ged Darod is a hundred times stronger. How can you, with your bone-barbed spears, hope to batter down its defenses?"

The Kings glared at him with their little stabbing eyes, sunk behind slabs of hard fat against eternities of wind.

Darik said, "How do we know this city exists?"

"Morn has been there. Let him show you."

Now they glared at Morn. But Astrane said, "Show us."

Morn nodded, summoning up the memories. Presently Stark could see again, in his own mind, the temples of Ged Darod with their shining roofs, the masses of people crowding the streets, the high bastion of the Upper City, which was the seat of the Wandsmen's power.

The Kings made grunting sounds and shook their heads. They would not show dismay.

"We are strong," they said. "We are fighters."

"You are savages," said Stark. "You have not seen the world for centuries. You could not fight it with nothing more than your courage, even if your numbers were great—and they are small. How many have you lost here, gaining nothing?"

He looked again at the wretched encampments of skin tents. And the Four Kings glared and said nothing, until Delbane spoke.

"We move north, regardless. But there may be truth in what you say."

"You need allies. Numbers. Weapons. As the spearhead of an army, you would be formidable. Iubar, too, moves north. You need her, she needs you. Make alliance. You will be serving only yourselves."

The warm wind blew. Streams of water blurred the faces of the ice-eyed kings who kept their long vigil in the cliffs of the berg. No one spoke.

Aud began suddenly to rant again, pounding his fists on his chest.

Delbane silenced him and asked Stark, "Do you promise us ships?"

"Somewhere along the way, surely."

Delbane nodded. "We will take counsel, the four of us."

22

As Gerrith had prophesied, Irnan was a dead city. Because of the siege, her fields had yielded no crops that year but corpses, and her people were dispersed among the other city-states to wait out the winter. The great gate hung open, and there was no one to oppose the Farers when they came.

These numbered fewer than a hundred, mostly stragglers from the great rout of the Farer army, and who because of fear or injuries had hidden in the hills instead of returning to Ged Darod with the bulk of the mob after the alien lightnings had barred their way to Irnan. There had been more of them. These were the survivors.

The cold had come upon them like a furtive enemy, long before its time. They suffered from hunger and the attacks of the Wild Bands. They shivered in their nakedness, in their faded body paint, in their inventive rags and tatters. The chill wind urged them south. They paused at Irnan only to see what pickings might be left there.

They passed along the tunnel through the thickness of the wall and came into the great square beyond. And they found that the city was not quite deserted.

A girl sat cross-legged on the platform that rose above the center of the square. It had been used for public executions, as was the custom, but the posts where once the victims were bound had been chopped away. The girl's dark hair covered her like a cloak, except where the wind lifted it to show her body painted in half-obliterated whorls of pink and silver, marred by time and rain and bramble scratches. Her eyes were closed, as if she slept.

A thin trickle of smoke rose from one of the buildings.

A man came out into the square, a muscular fellow clad in some burgher's cast-off robe. He had an indolent mouth and clever, mocking eyes, and he carried a drinking cup in his hand.

"Never mind her," he said to the newcomers. "She got kicked in the head at Tregad and she's daft ever since. My name is Wendor. Welcome to our city, and get your arses in out of the cold."

But the girl on the platform opened her eyes.

"It began here in Irnan," she said, and her voice echoed eerily from the walls. "They were the first traitors, these Irnanese. They wanted the ships to take them away. Because of them it all happened. Their wise woman made the prophecy about the Dark Man from the stars who would destroy the Lords Protector."

Her voice strengthened, ringing away along the narrow streets that opened into the square.

"I was here," she cried. "Here in this square. I saw the Dark Man bound on this platform, with the traitor Yarrod and the traitor Halk. I saw Yarrod die. How we tore his flesh when they threw him to us! I saw Gerrith, the daughter of Gerrith, stripped and bound in his place. I saw the elders of Irnan in chains. And then the arrows flew."

She stood up, flinging wide her arms. Wendor leaned himself in the doorway and sipped from his cup. The Farers shivered together but could not quite tear themselves away.

"From those windows the arrows flew. There, and there! They struck the Wandsman Mordach. Wandsmen and soldiers they slaughtered, and Farers—Farers! Us, the children of the Lords Protector. The arrows sang, and the cobbles were slippery with blood. They killed us and set the Dark Man free, to bring down the Citadel."

Her voice had risen to a harsh screaming, like the cries of a predatory bird.

From among the Farers, as she paused for breath, another voice spoke. "The Irnanese are beaten and the Dark Man most likely dead. Let us all go inside, girl, away from this wind."

She looked at them with mad eyes. "The Dark Man routed us at Tregad—"

"He had some help," Wendor said cynically, "from Delvor's army." He turned to the Farers. "Baya has this special feeling for the Dark Man, you see. At Skeg she betrayed him to the Wandsmen, but he survived. She tried to betray him again, but he caught her and carried her, a prisoner, almost to Irnan." He laughed. "I think she's in love with him."

"Give me a stone," screamed Baya. "Just one stone, that I may kill that vermin!"

"Come away in," said Wendor. "She'll be quiet when there's no one to listen."

The Farers flapped and shuffled across the square and through the doorway.

Wendor shouted at Baya. "Vermin, you call me, when I kept you alive all that time after Tregad, and you wandering in a daze? Vermin yourself! I don't care what you do. Burn the bloody city and yourself with it, if you want to, I've sat here long enough. I leave tomorrow."

He went inside.

Baya looked at the city and smiled, and said aloud, "Of course, burn it. That's why I came here."

She climbed down the steps from the platform, hugging herself. She felt the wind now.

It was warmer in the hall, where Wendor had made a fire of broken furniture. A cask of wine sat with its top stove in and Farers fighting to dip into it. Others were pulling down hangings wherewith to wrap themselves.

"The pigs left everything they couldn't carry," Wendor said. "All their old clothes, and the wine. Make yourselves free." He moved abruptly to haul Baya away from the fire, where she was setting an improvised torch alight. "Leave it! We're not quite finished with the city yet."

He cuffed her until he was sure she understood.

Baya wandered off. She found odds and ends of clothing and put them on, taking pleasure in the chill emptiness of rooms and passages, desolate places that had once been homes. She shouted defiant obscenities to the hollow spaces, in which Stark's name was prominently echoed. "Beaten, beaten, beaten!" she cried. "And where is your strength now, Dark Man? Mother Skaith was too strong for you. *We* were too strong for you!"

She ran out of breath at last, and began to search for food. The Irnanese had left little enough of that behind them. Still, she found a smoked joint forgotten in a cupboard, and only partly gnawed by the small creatures who had found it first; and after that a cheese. She filled her mouth and went on her way, munching, carrying the food in her looped-up skirt.

In one kitchen she found a flint-and-steel, and, in a dark stores room, lamp oil. Smiling, she gathered together a heap of debris, of hangings and furniture, and splashed oil over it; then she set herself industriously to make sparks.

For a while Baya warmed herself, watching the flames lick up and catch in the wooden ceiling. When hot ash began to fall on her, she went away into the narrow street. Back in the square she climbed up on the platform again and sat herself down. She ate some more while the smoke rose above the roofs, thinly at first, then more sturdily until it was a black and ever-widening pillar against the sky.

The wind helped.

When night came on, she could see the flames. She was still sitting there, watching, when Wendor and the others, roused from wine-heavy sleep by each other's coughing, staggered out of the smoky hall. By now the square was illumined by a red glare. Flames danced, roaring, over the rooftops.

Wendor climbed the platform. He picked up what was left of the joint and the cheese and threw them to the others, then he picked up Baya and carried her down the steps and through the gate. He beat her all the way, but she only watched the flames and smiled.

Irnan burned for seven days.

It made a great smoke; but Kazimni of Izvand, riding at the head of a troop of two hundred warriors, was too far away to see it, though it would have brought him pleasure. He and his mercenaries had twice suffered defeat there, first as garrison at the time of the revolt, and then as assault troops at the siege, all in the service of the Wandsmen. He knew Stark well. He had given the off-worlder safe-conduct as far as Izvand and then sold him to Amnir of Komrey for a good sum, to be resold to the Lords Protector. He had been amazed and respectful when Stark turned up alive to raise the siege of Irnan. Now surely the Dark Man was dead, and more pressing matters occupied Kazimni. Matters such as starvation and survival.

They had come east from Izvand across the Barrens, plundering where they could, with scant profit. They crossed the Border in frost and hail and came down on Tregad. But Tregad's walls were thick and her home bands well-trained. Kazimni poked and prodded, hoping for a weak spot. He found none and took his men off toward Ged Darod.

"In these times," he said, "the Wandsmen will likely have need of us. And in any case, we won't go hungry."

Folk would go hungry in Izvand that winter. He thought of his beloved city beside the frozen Sea of Skorva, and his hard jaw tightened. If what the wise men said was true, and the Goddess had set her hand on Izvand, then that city's day was done. He remembered Stark and his talk of better worlds beyond the sky, and he remembered his own answer. "The land shapes us. If we were in another place, we would be another people." The Izvandians had chosen, at the time of the Wandering, to remain on the edge of winter, in a climate similar to that of their original home farther north. Now it seemed that they might well be forced to move again, and the thought was a black one to Kazimni.

Yet he did not shirk it. If it were so, other folk would likewise be forced south, and much blood was bound to flow as they fought each other for land. It was better to be in the vanguard, to take first and hold on.

He thought of Ged Darod and its temples crammed with treasure, and he wondered secretly if the Wandsmen had not outlived their usefulness.

To the north, other men moved down along the Wandsmen's Road. There had been a drawing of lots at Yurunna, based upon the amount of food available. Those who drew the black pebbles were now upon their way, with their families and possessions, hooded tribesmen in dusty cloaks of the six colors, fierce blue eyes showing above their veils and weapons at their belts. Behind them came the Tarf, enclosing within their green-gold ranks the hundreds of the Fallarin with folded wings, perched on tall desert beasts and looking forward savagely to a future in an unknown land.

Far behind, ignored in their orange cloaks, came the remnants of the once-proud Ochar, First-Come of Kheb, who had broken their might upon their own ambition.

The army marched on its way. In the low desert, frost had dimmed the reptilian colors of sand and rock, and in the debatable lands beyond the trees were hung with funeral draperies of dead leaves, which dropped steadily before a keening wind. Every pond was frozen.

Foraging parties found no food. Packs of starving wanderers attacked them for their own flesh. Wild Bands, subhuman creatures who knew no law but hunger, leaped at their throats from ambush. The men from the north pulled their girdles tighter and hastened south, keeping to the road because it was easy and well-marked.

The stations of the Keepers of the Middle Road were abandoned. Since the fall of Yurunna, the Wandsmen had had no occasion to travel this far. Their boundaries were drawing in, around the warm plain of Ged Darod.

23

The Kings of the White Islands found their ships at last, and not a day too soon.

Progress had been rapid enough earlier, but not easy. The Islanders, tireless on their ice floes, were unused to hill-climbing. They became sore-footed and irritable. There were quarrels and killings, and only the cruel hands of the Four Kings held them from tribal warfare.

Several hundred of the people of Iubar had been forced to march by land as well, because there was not room for them in their ships. They, too, were sore-footed and irritable, and they suffered from the steady diet of fish, which they insisted on cooking. Nothing was available from the land, and scurvy plagued them, as did the dysentery common to camps. Daily halts were made for burial parties. The Islanders ate everything raw, and throve. They became increasingly impatient with the Iubarians, threatening to go on alone and leave them to their misery.

Stark and Halk spent much time trying to hold the ill-mated force together. Stark was a grim and silent man these days, and even Halk walked wide of him. Gerd and Grith were ever at his heels, and the whole pack followed when he went among the ranks.

Morn was Stark's liaison with the ships of Iubar, and the situation there was worsening with each rising of Old Sun. Over-crowded and deep-laden as they were, the ships could still outdistance the marchers on land,

and must needs heave to and wait, lest they lose touch entirely.

There is sickness aboard, said Morn one day. *It costs my people much effort to find food for so many. Water becomes a problem. There is fear, and much discontent. The Lady Sanghalain is told by her advisers to forget the promise of star-ships and sail on to seek new land for her people, abandoning those on shore. They care nothing for the Islanders.*

They will, said Stark, *when they need them to fight. And what about the Iubarians here, Sanghalain's own folk?*

There are those who say that they must be sacrificed for the good of the rest. One day, she will have to listen.

Stark did not need to be told how near this shaky alliance was to breaking up. He could feel it, as a man feels quicksand beneath his feet.

So, when Morn brought word of a fortified town ahead, and a harbor filled with ships, he took the news at once to the Four Kings where they marched beneath the gold-bright Head of Gengan.

Aud showed his large, strong teeth. "Now," he said, "we shall see how the Dark Man fights."

It was a simple operation, swiftly done.

The Irnanese had chosen to march by land, with Halk. All the rest were in the boat, which did not sail in company with the ships of Iubar but stayed closer inshore, in constant touch with Stark. Now the tribesmen and the Fallarin and Tarf, except those necessary to crew the boat, joined the land forces, glad of something to do.

Leaving Halk in charge, Stark and Tuchvar ranged ahead with the hounds in two separate parties, to locate any landward guardposts. The Northhounds found and silenced them before the watchers were aware of any force approaching through the thick woods with their curtain of frost-blighted leaves.

From a ridge of high ground, Stark looked down at the town.

It seemed cramped within a ditch and palisade. Probably it had grown too rapidly, as lost and landless people accreted around the strong leader whose crude banner hung above the gate—a tanned hide with a splash of color on it, indistinguishable at this distance. Some of the buildings were old. Others were new or still in the making, and many were rough shelters of boughs and skins.

In the small, crowded harbor were craft much like the one Stark's people used, designed alike for fishing and for battle. A number of these had been stripped and supplied with mechanisms that had nothing to do with fishing. Most of the half-dozen coasting traders moored along the outer quay at the far side of the harbor were probably prizes captured by the refitted boats. The quay itself, like the houses of the original village, was old, a rough construction of logs and stones.

People moved in the streets of the town. There was a market. The hammers of builders rang. Along the harbor front fishermen mended nets, and among the boats a scattering of men repaired rigging or banged away at carpentry.

On a small island, little more than a hump of rock beside the harbor mouth stood a tumbledown tower with a mangonel on top and some armed men lounging about. A narrow causeway led from the tower to the end of the quay, and people were fishing from it with hand lines. Some sort of ordered life had found a footing here and was resuming its normal patterns. It seemed a pity to break them up again, but there was no help for it and the damage ought not to be irreparable, no more than a severe shaking-up.

Stark looked at the sky. Then he went back down from the ridge to where the army waited. By the sea's edge he conferred with the Four Kings and with his own leaders, and with Morn, and presently Morn slipped into the tideless water and disappeared, heading for Sanghalain's ships, which lay out of sight beyond a headland.

Stark said to the Four Kings, "Pick your men." He turned to Aud. "You and I will march together."

Aud smiled. "Where are your very powerful weapons, Dark Man?"

"They're not needed here," Stark said. "Unless you would feel safer?"

Aud snarled, and went to collect his force.

They set off through the woods, making a long circle around the town. The hounds ran ahead as before, to clear the way. They were excited, impatient for battle. They growled and whimpered, and their minds were filled with sparks of fire.

Stark's mind, like his heart, was filled with blackness. He needed the release of battle even more than the hounds, before that which was inside him should overwhelm him. He led the long line of Islanders—Aud's and Astrane's—among the blighted trees, going fast, with a morose and savage face that made Aud think better of his taunts.

Old Sun dropped over the edge of the world before they had completed their circuit.

In darkness, Stark led the way down toward the harbor side. They waited among the trees, where scrub woods covered a slope above the water. Gerd and Grith pressed close to Stark, panting, and he laid his hands on them as the first of the Three Ladies rose in the northern sky. Stark's eyes caught the light and shone like ice, whereas the eyes of the hounds were hot and yellow.

The palisade gate was shut. The town was remarkably quiet, showing few lights. The sentries the hounds had slain must have been found by now. Stark wondered what the leaders had made of them, being dead with no mark on them except the look of fear, and whether they knew about the army so close at hand. Certainly they would be alert and on guard. The only surprises would be in the method of attack and the size of the forces involved—which would not include the Iubarian marchers, who were far behind.

The second of the Three Ladies rose. The harbor

water gleamed pure silver, the dark hulls and masts in sharp silhouette against it. The only lamps were in the island tower at the end of the quay, a few vagrant yellow rays showing through arrow-slits and cracks in the masonry.

The Islanders were as still as couching beasts. Stark could hear their breathing, and the rough panting of the hounds. He listened beyond these sounds, stretching his hearing against the outer silence, and all at once he heard a small splashing, as though a fish had jumped, close by the tower.

Dark shapes broke the quiet silver. They were all around the tower, on the causeway, rushing the inner defenses. A man screamed, and the night shattered into barbs of sound.

Stark said, "Be ready."

The Islanders gathered themselves, a faint rustling among the trees.

Voices shouted in the town. A flat-toned drum pounded and a horn blew.

More dark shapes appeared on the quay. Their wet hides glistened as they busied themselves among the mooring lines.

"Now," said Stark. And Astrane's men went, with a crackling of leaves, straight for the quay, where they would guard the Ssussminh.

The town gates burst open. Armed men rushed out, heading for the harbor.

"Now!" Stark shouted to Aud, and ran from the woods with the Northhounds baying before him.

The townsmen turned to fight. Stark saw a jostling of hard leathery faces in the gentle light, and a brandishing of weapons. He heard screaming as the hounds killed. Then he was in the midst of it.

He was only dimly aware of Aud fighting beside him, silent and deadly. The Islanders never made a sound, either of challenge or pain, and he felt something eerie in that voiceless ferocity that contrasted with the shouts and cries of the townsmen, who outnumbered the

Islanders but who quickly became uncertain whether they were fighting men or trolls.

Nevertheless, the townsmen fought fiercely, until the other part of the army came pouring down the cliffs and took them in flank. Then they retreated, running in panic for the gate until a powerfully built man with a mane of yellow hair roared and rallied them and beat the Islanders back. Stark crossed blades with him briefly, and then the fighting swept them apart. A few minutes later, the townsmen were shut inside their palisade again and Stark stood shivering and sweating while the hounds fed around him. Aud looked at him once, then turned away.

The small army leaned on its spears and waited until the coasting ships and a sufficient number of smaller craft had been towed or worked out of the harbor, with the aid of the Ssussminh, the Fallarin putting a breath of wind in the sails. Sanghalain's larger ships now stood off the harbor mouth to discourage pursuit by sea. The Islanders withdrew, making their way back to the shore, and the gates of the town remained closed.

The lengthy process of embarkation began.

When the last of the Islanders and Iubarians were safely crammed away somehow in the captured craft, Stark returned to his own boat and slept for a long time. When he awoke, the strange look was gone from him, and Ashton was at pains to hide his relief.

The ships sailed in company, in two separate wings that did not intermix. They made good speed with a following wind. Old Sun's rusty fires burned hotter with each day. At night the Three Ladies mounted higher overhead, their brilliance echoed in the phosphorescent wakes. It was necessary to put into shore for water, and often there was fighting. At sea, predatory sails showed from time to time, and then sheered off when both the size and poverty of the fleet became evident.

Pedrallon put off his furs and ceased to shiver.

Neither the Iubarians nor the Ssussminh had any use for the rotting tropics, and in any case these were already beleaguered, crowded with refugees from both

north and south and violently disinclined to welcome
any more. It seemed that Sanghalain had no choice but
to go on to Ged Darod, in hopes of the star-ship that
Gerrith had promised.

But all that way north across the Great Sea to Skeg,
the radio gave not even the faintest whisper of a human
voice. They heard only the far-off hiss and crackle of
star-talk, where the great suns spoke among themselves
of things unknowable to man.

Stark could not imagine that Gerrith would have lied
to him, but in her state of exalted self-deception she
might have believed anything. Prophecies were slippery
things, blades to turn in the believer's hand and pierce
him. Stark looked at Old Sun and knew that the ginger
star was like to be the only sun that he and Simon
Ashton would ever see.

And then that happened which made him think that,
after all, Gerrith might have seen true things in her
Water of Vision.

A sudden tropic storm struck the fleet. Its brief
violence did for several of the smaller craft, and
Stark's was among them. Her mast went by the board
and her sprung seams took water so rapidly that there
was no time to save anything but their lives. Transceivers and automatics went to the bottom, leaving
them as Gerrith had said—mute, and with nothing of
the off-worlds left in their hands.

The need to reach Ged Darod quickly became like
a fever that ran through all ranks. Ferdias now
possessed the only voice on Skaith that could be heard
beyond the sky.

24

The highest vantage point of the Upper City of Ged
Darod was a marble kiosk atop the Palace of the
Twelve, where members of the Council might sit, if
they chose, and look out over their domain.

Ferdias and the five other Lords Protector—old
Gorrel was on his deathbed—stood here with the wind
stirring their white hair and snowy robes. They stared
out over the Lower City to the gray-green plain, laced
with the ribbons of the pilgrim roads which came
from every direction to converge upon Ged Darod.
Each northerly road spawned its own dustcloud, perpetually rising.

"Is there no end to them?" asked Ferdias.

It was too far to distinguish individual characteristics,
but Ferdias had seen the pilgrims at closer range than
this, and he knew that too few of them were in fact
pilgrims—visitors who would make their offerings in
the temples and then go away again. Too many were
refugees, bringing carts piled high with belongings and
old people and children, victims of the Goddess seeking help from the Wandsmen. Ferdias would not have
believed that the hills and valleys of the North Temperate Zone contained so large a population, or that
one season's crop failure could create such widespread
destitution. Of course, the Wandsmen's tithes took a
fair portion of the surplus, so that little was left for
hoarding. But even so . . .

The streets and hostels of the Lower City were full.

Camps had sprung up outside the walls, and they grew larger by the day.

"We must have more supplies," said Ferdias.

"The north has no more to give, my lord," said one of the red-robed Wandsmen who stood behind with their wands of office.

"I am aware of that. But the south has suffered no killing frosts. There are fish in the sea—"

"There is great disruption in the south," said another red-clad Wandsman. "The whole pattern of distribution has changed. There are many refugees, twice as many people to be fed, either by trade or rapine. Our requests are refused, or evaded. Wandsmen have been attacked. The southern princes tell us that the needs of their own people must be met before any other."

"Our fisheries," said a third Wandsman, "have been much disturbed by the movements of the Children of the Sea, who demand their own tribute."

"Yet these people here at Ged Darod must be fed," said Ferdias, with an edge of iron in his voice. "I have before me now a full inventory of the contents of our storehouses in both the upper and the lower cities. Even with the strictest rationing, which is not practical, a month would see the end of our supplies." He swept his hand wide in a gesture that took in the city, the plain, and all living things therein. "How will it be, do you think, when they come to our table and find it bare?"

The red Wandsmen, members of the Twelve with their pride and their gold-tipped wands, looked everywhere but at Ferdias. And he thought that he could see fear peeping out of their eyes.

"They will go elsewhere," one of them said.

"They will not go elsewhere. For two thousand years we have taught them not to go elsewhere. We are their hope and their promise. If we fail them—"

"There are the mercenaries."

"Shall we use them against our children? And besides," Ferdias added, "who can say where their loyalties will be when their own bellies pinch?"

Softly the myriad bells tinkled on the peacock roofs of the temples below. On the other side of the thousand-windowed building that rose like a white cliff above those roofs, the inner courts and cloisters of the Wandsmen's city basked in the sunlight. Ferdias thought of the Citadel, and of Yurunna, and the withering-away of great power; and it was almost as though the man Stark had somehow induced the Dark Goddess to favor him, so that they moved hand in hand across the planet to destroy everything the Wandsmen had labored so long to build.

"Do you not see?" said Ferdias to the twelve Wandsmen. "These people must be fed!"

Kazimni of Izvand was thinking along much the same lines.

A portion of the pleasure gardens in the lower city had been set aside for the mercenaries to make their camps. And other troops besides the Izvandians had come to Ged Darod seeking food and employment. A sea of Farers milled around them, occasionally lapping over their boundaries. The mercenaries policed their camps. The Farers did not. The stench of the once-beautiful gardens was overpowering, and it was no better in the streets.

Facilities that had been ample, over the centuries, for the normal influx of pilgrims and wintering Farers were inadequate to cope with the unprecedented numbers of people who ate and slept and performed their bodily functions wherever they could find room. The hospital and the crèche were overrun. Even the temples were not spared. The Wandsmen and their servitors did what they could, but outbreaks of disease had begun in the city and in the refugee camps outside. Distribution of food to the multitudes was slow and difficult. There were fist-shakings and screams of complaint, and sometimes small riots in which supply carts were forcibly taken. Increasingly, the mercenaries were called in to keep order. And increasingly, the over-stretched fabric began to crack.

Walking guard with his men to protect the supply carts, or lying at night in the camp with the breathing, stirring, stinking mob around him close enough to touch, Kazimni could feel the city as a tangible weight that could easily move and crush him. He knew now that he had not been wise to come here—no wiser, in fact, than the Wandsmen had been to reject the starships. He considered what he ought to do when the bounty of the Wandsmen was used up, and his gaze turned often to the white pile of the Upper City.

Far out on the plain, a mad-eyed girl in faded body paint of pink and silver danced in the dust of the western road, on the way to Ged Darod.

In a defile of the mountains, the People of the Towers had halted in their line of march. There were not as many of them as there had been when they left the Darklands. Degenerate creatures lairing in the dead cities of the north had taken a toll. So had the long, cold journey itself, and not always of the weakest. They traveled light now, having eaten all their beasts. What they had left of supplies were easily carried. Their gaunt and narrow bodies, clad all in close-fitting gray, were narrower than ever, so that they looked like a company of ghosts moving through the snow squalls on the mountain's flanks. Now they stood still, not knowing why, weapons ready, pallid eyes alert behind the holes of their tight gray masks, most of which were unmarked by any sign of rank. They waited, children and adults alike, without question or complaint.

At the head of the line, Hargoth the Corn-King, with the stylized wheat-ears worked on his mask, stood facing a band of women.

They had appeared out of the veils of snow to bar the way, and their only garment was a kind of black bag that covered the head. Their naked bodies were scraggy and lean, and the skin of them was like the bark of old trees, roughened by many seasons of exposure.

The foremost among them cried out in a harsh,

creaking voice that Old Sun was dying. The other women echoed her, wailing. They tossed their arms skyward and turned their hidden faces to the dim glow of the ginger star among the storm clouds.

"Blood," screamed the woman. "Strength. Fire. There are no men left upon the mountains, and Old Sun starves."

"What do you want of us?" asked Hargoth, though he knew very well what they wanted, and he glanced quickly upward at the steep sides of the defile, where bark-brown shapes lurked behind boulders, ready to push them down. He made a sign with his fingers, but it was not needed. His sorcerer-priests were moving quietly behind him into the ritual pattern of the Calling. Behind the priests, a man with twin lightning strokes on his mask was passing whispered orders to men who carried javelins.

Hargoth extended his arm. With his priests standing now in a half-circle at his back, he was like the point of an arrow nocked on a bowstring. The power of the linked minds joined to his began to pour through him, channeled and directed as he chose.

"Tell me what it is you want."

"Life," said the foremost woman. "Life to pour out sweetly for our lord and brother. We are the Sisters of the Sun. We serve him, keeping him strong with his proper food. Give us, that we may feed him."

"I, too, worship Old Sun," said Hargoth softly. His eyes shone through the holes of his mask, bits of winter sky, chill and colorless. "I also worship the Three, my lord Darkness and his lady Cold and their daughter Hunger. They tread close upon my heels, little sister. Can you not feel the breath of the Goddess, bringing you peace?"

The cold had become intense. A rime of frost settled on the women. Falling snow clung to it, ice to ice. The air was full of tiny sounds, cracklings and tinklings as though the air itself froze and fell.

Up on the slopes groans and cries could be heard where flying javelins found their mark. A single boulder came crashing down, missing by a hair two priests who scrambled from its path. The pattern was broken and so was the force of the linked minds that had willed the cold. But that single thrust had been enough. Tree-bark bodies lay still, or feebly tossed their scrawny limbs. Others who had not received the full gift of the Goddess crept away whimpering into the forest.

"Let us go on," said Hargoth. And the long gray line began to move again, quietly through the snow.

It came down out of the mountains at length, into a valley where abandoned plowlands glistened like dark metal with the frost. A city sat on a height of land, a burnt-out shell drifted with ash. Still, much of it could be made habitable again, and the climate was mild. There was some talk of stopping here. But there was nothing to eat, so the talk died quickly.

Hargoth cast the finger-bones of the Spring Child. Three times he cast them, and three times they pointed to the east. The People of the Towers went on, along the northern flank of a mountain range much higher than the one they had just traversed, its peaks hidden in thick cloud.

The men of Thyra marched more slowly, bearing their heavy weight of iron in solid ranks that ground relentlessly onward, with Strayer's Hammer at the fore. Within their clanking lines were the women and children and beasts of burden. They halted only when attacked, and then their iron swords and shields swung outward in a deadly defensive wall.

Because they lacked the cunning and the ghost-footed swiftness of Hargoth's people, they were attacked much more often. At Izvand they dallied, scenting food in plenty behind the walls. But the gates were too stout for their battering. They ate the last of their beasts and passed on.

Crossing the Barrens, they forced their way through the mountains, treading down the snow in the passes. When they came at last into the warm lands of the south, with green things growing on every side, they had lost above a hundred of their original number, not counting women and children. Enervated now by the heat, weakened by the long journey, sweating and chafing in their iron mail, they tramped on in search of food.

A dim path led them to a clearing where half a dozen thatched huts stood and half a dozen families were winnowing their small crop of grain. The farmers died swiftly.

The Thyrans rested and fed full. On the third day, a Wandsman in a green robe and a ten of armed mercenaries came looking for a share of the harvested grain.

They were surrounded before they knew it. They were brought to where the Ironmaster sat, with Strayer's banner beside him and Strayer's Hammer in dark metal upon his breast.

"Tell me," he said, "where I may find Gelmar of Skeg."

The Wandsman was young, and he was frightened, looking at the swords. "There is not so much iron in all the Fertile Belt," he said. "You must come from far away."

"From Thyra, close to the Citadel. We took captives for Gelmar once, a red-haired woman and some others from Irnan, and a man who was said to have come from the stars. Gelmar paid us well. Perhaps he will help us now. We seek a place where we may set up our forges again, away from the Dark Goddess who takes the strength from iron. Where may we find Gelmar?"

Gelmar was at Ged Darod, but the Wandsman lied because there were already too many folk there to be fed.

"He is at Skeg," he said, and told the Ironmaster how he might come there. "Now," he said, "I see that you have already eaten most of the grain, so I will go my way."

But he did not go anywhere, and he never knew the fruits of his lies.

25

The ships made landfall by Skeg. The two wings divided, Stark's wing going to the north and Sanghalain's to the south, so that Skeg could be attacked by land from two sides, with the Ssussminh coming in from the harbor. The action was badly timed, so that Stark and his force joined Morn in the wreckage of the marketplace and had the town well in hand before the first of Sanghalain's men showed up.

Fortunately there was little opposition. With the burning of the spaceport and the foreign enclave, Skeg had sunk back again to the status of a small port dealing lethargically in fish and grain. Most of the inhabitants ran for their lives and were not pursued. A brief, hot skirmish took place at the fishery, where a troop of mercenaries stood guard against raiders and protected the Wandsman who claimed most of the catch. The Wandsman was taken alive.

Stark questioned him, about Ged Darod.

"All is well there," said the Wandsman. His face was strained, and he would not meet Stark's eye. "There are ten thousand ready fighting men, and twice that number in reserve—"

Lies, said Gerd, and lifted his lip on one side to show part of a row of fangs.

Touch him.

Gerd's eyes glowed. The Wandsman sank down to his knees, sobbing.

"I will ask you again," said Stark. "How is it in Ged Darod?"

182

The Wandsman was middle-aged. He had memories. He looked at Stark with black hatred and said nothing.

Touch him.

Gerd touched, flicking the whip of terror across the Wandsman's mind.

"They come," said the Wandsman, stammering. "From everywhere they come, the hungry and the homeless, and we"—he bent his head and shivered— "we cannot feed them all. When the food is gone . . . I do not know. Their faces terrify me. It is the end of us, I think."

"Are there no troops? Mercenaries? Surely the Upper City is defended."

"Defended? Oh, yes. And there are mercenaries. And many others who will fight. But once we have failed our people, once they have lost faith in us—"

"You failed them when you sent the ships away," Stark said. "And now the Goddess is bringing home the truth. I'm minded to make an offering to her when we reach Ged Darod." He turned to the captain of the Iubarians and said quietly, "I advise you to be a little more prompt next time. If the Islanders should come to believe that you're deliberately sending them in ahead to do your fighting for you, you may have some unpleasantness to deal with."

"Hold the brutes back then, if you can," said the captain. "We'll not run to catch up!"

He went away with his men to establish a defense perimeter, which was held while supplies were unloaded from the ships and the war engines brought ashore piecemeal to be prepared for the march.

No attacks came. During the delay, Stark scouted the countryside with the Islanders to keep them busy. They were tight-coiled, savagely impatient now that the promised land was just beyond the horizon. Stark knew how they felt: every laggard hour was torture to him, wondering if the rescue ship had come, and if Ferdias was in touch with it. Stark had feared that the Islanders would wilt in the heat. Instead they had bloomed, stripping away their furs, offering their pale bodies to the sun until they were as dark as teakwood. They went about near naked now, men and women both, charged with a vitality that was almost frightening. The Four Kings fingered the gold plaques around their necks, their eyes turned always to the northeast.

The Ssussminh did not fare so well. They hid their bodies from the drying sun that cracked their skin. They moved heavily on land, and the heat seemed to sap their strength, though they were still formidable enough. Nevertheless, they did not complain. But whenever Stark was near them his mind was aware of sadness, and he "saw" things that he had never seen with his own eyes: the halls and chambers of a city beneath the sea, beautiful with pearls and coral and ivory and many-colored shells. He walked in the streets of that city, and he watched it die as the dark seawater flooded in; and he felt the terrible regret, the yearning after things forever lost.

In what was really a very short time, though it seemed like an eternity, the army took the Wandsmen's Road and went north, traveling as fast as men might travel, dragging catapults and the great war engines on wheeled carts built for them by ship's carpenters during the voyage. The women of Iubar, who did not bear arms, remained behind with their children and a strong guard in the old fortress beside Skeg harbor. No one knew what would happen at Ged Darod. Only Sanghalain went with the fighting men, surrounded by tall Ssussminh who carried her in a chair with long poles, which they set upon their shoulders.

Stark's own small company went ahead of all, even before the Head of Gengan. Alderyk, who had turned broody and ill-tempered as a falcon in moult, was as impatient as the Islanders.

"My people are somewhere on this road. It was a mad dream that made me leave them."

"You came to control the whirlwind," Stark said, "so that it should not do too great damage to your world. Remember?"

"A fool's reason. I was led by my own desire to see

more of that world. The Place of Winds was a prison. Now that my people have been forced to leave it, it seems incalculably beautiful and precious."

"The Goddess has claimed it. You can never go back."

"And where shall we go, Dark Man? Where shall we find another home?"

"If a ship comes, as Gerrith promised—"

"I am weary of this talk of ships."

Alderyk's wings spread and snapped shut again with a vicious crack. Dust sprang up from the road in a whirling cloud.

Halk laughed. "We are all weary of your ships, Dark Man, and of Gerrith's prophecies. We can trust to nothing now but our own strong hands." The hilt of the great sword glittered in the sun above his left shoulder. He said softly to Stark, "I have not forgotten my pledge to you."

"Nor have I," Stark answered angrily. "How is it that a child can grow so tall?" He strode away, taking his growling, bristling hounds with him.

It was while he scouted ahead with the pack that he received Gerd's warning. *Men!* And a little later he saw the dark mass of them barring the way.

The Ironmaster's folk had gone aside from the direct path to Skeg in search of food. They found a guard station on the Wandsmen's road and took it. Both men and beasts were there, for these stations on the Lower Road were still maintained, and the Ironmaster was well pleased.

Until the army came upon him.

At first sight of the dust, the shield-wall formed. Women hastily piled human carcasses on the beasts of burden. The Ironmaster stood beneath Strayer's wind-whipped banner, waiting.

The army halted. Stark looked at the banner. At first he did not believe what he saw. But then the glint of dark iron from the rows of shields and caps and breastplates left no doubt.

"Thyrans," he said.

Halk, who had come up with him, reached his two hands to the longsword and brought it singing out of its scabbard.

"I remember them." He lifted the sword high. He shouted to the Islanders and plunged forward.

Stark kicked Halk's feet from under him and knocked him flat with a blow across the back of the neck. *Hold him,* he said to the hounds, and picked up the sword.

The Islanders had begun to move, eager for battle. Stark shouted to the Four Kings, "Call them back!"

Delbane said, "We do not fear their swords and shields."

"There's no need for such haste. Halk has a personal quarrel with these people, who killed his shield-mate. Unless they attack us, let be until I talk to them."

Morn had come up to see what was the matter. Stark spoke to him briefly and he went back to the Iubarians. Then Stark glanced at Halk, lying fire-eyed in the dust with the pack around him, and called to Gerd and Grith. He walked forward toward the Iron-master.

"The last time we met," said Stark, "was in your house at Thyra, when you sold me and my people to the Wandsmen."

The Ironmaster nodded. He looked at the North-hounds. "We heard that you had stolen the guardians of the Citadel. We did not quite believe." He shrugged, and the hammer symbol lifted on his thick chest. "So. You outnumber us, and you have the deathhounds. Still, we can fight." The iron ranks crashed blades on shields. "Or you can let us go on our way peacefully to Skeg."

"What do you hope to find at Skeg?"

"The Wandsman Gelmar. We need a new place to build our forges, beyond reach of the Goddess. He may help us."

"Gelmar is not there. Few are there now except Iubarian women and children." He looked past the Ironmaster and the soldiers to where the laden beasts stood with the arms and legs of their burdens dangling down. "You will understand why we can't permit you to go to Skeg."

"What, then?"

"The Wandsmen's day is done. Come with us to Ged Darod and help finish it."

"We have no quarrel with the Wandsmen. We want—"

"—a place to build your forges. It will have to be on another world, then. You have more metal on your backs than has been seen in the Fertile Belt for a thousand years, and you'll find no city here like Thyra. The Wandsmen can give you nothing."

"That is only your word," said the Ironmaster. "The word of an outlander."

"It is the only word you have," Stark told him. "Join with us, or we will crush you."

The Ironmaster considered. There were many men, and not-men. Archers had moved out to the flanks. A strange machine was being trundled up. Battle now, against these odds, would mean the destruction of his people as an entity, no matter if some of them did survive. He looked up at the banner above him.

"Perhaps it is Strayer's will," he said. "So be it."

"You'll march with me," said Stark, appreciating the simplicity of one-man rule, where no time need be wasted haggling with committees. The Ironmaster spoke, and it was done. "Remember that the North-hounds can hear your thoughts. If there is treachery, you will be the first to die."

The Thyran men, in two parties, were sent out to take point on either side. The Thyran women, their children, and their laden beasts with their grisly burdens—decently covered, for neither the Iubarians nor the Islanders were man-eaters and both considered the habit gross—were placed in the center of the line.

Stark returned the longsword to Halk. Nothing more was said on either side. But Stark put two of the hounds to watch at Halk's back.

The Ironmaster's standard-bearer came with him to

Stark's side. The army moved on again—a long, fat, motley-colored snake winding along the dusty road.

"How was it with Hargoth and his people?" asked Stark.

"The Gray Ones had already fled. We never saw them." The Ironmaster shrugged. "Perhaps the Goddess devoured them all."

The long miles fell behind. One by one, the stations were overwhelmed. And on a hot noonday they came to the plain of Ged Darod, where Stark pointed out the roofs of the city a-glitter in the sunlight.

The Four Kings stepped forward beneath the golden Head of Gengan. They knelt and touched the ground with their hands.

Stark looked up sidelong at the rusty blaze of Old Sun. *Your favor was bought dearly,* he said, but only the hounds heard him, and whined. *I hope the taste of her blood was sweet. Be patient, I will give you more.*

The Islanders did what he had known they would do. They broke from the line of march, disdaining orders, forgetting everything but the sight of their ancient home. Like a company of tigers, they bounded out across the plain.

Ashton shouted, "Eric!"

But he was gone, running with the Islanders and the white hounds, leaving the Thyrans and the men of Iubar to follow as they would.

26

The sun was hot on his face. He smelled sweat and dust; the animal smell of the Islanders; the coarse, hairy reek of the hounds. He ran, and the sword in his hand was bright.

People scattered from the pilgrim roads. The many-gated walls of Ged Darod rose above the plain, and the gates were open. They were always open. But now the heavy valves were stuttering to and fro. The army had been seen, the order given to shut the gates that had not been shut for centuries. Those within struggled to obey. But from the huddled camps without the walls came panic mobs to push the other way, lest they be barred out and left to the mercy of the foe.

Stark yelled—a high, strange cry that startled even the Islanders, a cry that belonged far away on another world where snouted half-men urged each other on to the kill. The Northhounds bayed, a deep-mouthed sinister belling.

One gate of all the gates, the nearest one, became the focal point of their rush. People were locked there in a single, swaying mass that broke and fragmented before them, shredding away at the edges, falling beneath swords and spears and the killer-minds of the hounds.

No firm resistance was met. One small band of mercenaries fought determinedly but were soon disposed of. The others—Farers, pilgrims, refugees—simply ran. The Islanders had scarcely lost momentum. With great difficulty Stark held them until Ashton and part of his own troop came up, the Thyrans clanking

189

after them, grunting and puffing. The Fallarin had drawn aside with their Tarf to sit out the messy business; there was nothing much they could do in a battle of this kind.

Stark saw that the Iubarians were coming, for once on the double, except for the men who hauled the catapults. He detailed a force of Thyrans to secure the gate and then ran on again with the Islanders—Irnanese and tribesmen at his back and Halk's long sword swinging. The balance of the Ironmaster's force tramped heavily behind, a moving shield-wall bristling with swordpoints.

Pedrallon alone bore no weapon. Himself a Wandsman of high rank before his downfall, this had been his city, where he walked in pride and power. Stark wondered what his thoughts must be as he walked here now, seeing what had happened to Ged Darod.

For much had happened.

Buildings were in flames. Storehouses had been plundered. The temples with their peacock roofs had been sacked, even the golden Sun Temple, where bodies were scattered on the steps. Dead priests and Wandsmen floated in the sacred tank. Ragtag mobs ran this way and that, disorganized gobbets of fear and fury. They did not present much of a threat, but Stark knew that mercenary troops were in Ged Darod, and he wondered why they did not appear.

The stench of the streets rose about them in the heat. Delbane spat and said, "Our land has been defiled."

Darik answered, "It shall be cleansed."

Gerd growled. *Death, N'Chaka. Men fight. Kill.*

Stark nodded. He had already heard the distant voice of war.

Again he restrained the Four Kings, all but beating them back to give the Thyrans time to close up. He felt nervous in the narrow streets, which compressed and diminished his effective force.

He led on toward the roar of the mob, because that was where they had to go.

They came out into the vast square below the Upper City. It was packed with people, a surging multitude that beat like surf against the white cliff that reared above with its rows of small, secret windows. The outer portions of the mob were Farers and refugees, armed with whatever makeshift weapons they could lay their hands on. Up front, and leading the assault, were the mercenaries; and now Stark understood why they had not bothered to defend the city. They were clustered on and around the dais from which the Wandsmen had used to speak to their people, and there were more of them in the tunneled gate above, where ceremonial steps ran upward, out of sight. From deep within this tunnel came the muffled booming of a ram.

"What are these people doing?" asked Delbane.

"That is the sacred enclave of the city. They want to take it."

The mob had begun to turn and face the new threat. The mercenaries, from their higher vantage point, had also become aware of them. Stark saw a sudden flurry of activity around the tunnel mouth. Tough, well-disciplined ranks began to form.

"But we must have it for ourselves," said Delbane. "Is that not so?"

"That is so," Stark answered, looking at the overwhelming mob and the monolithic wall beyond it.

"Well, then . . ." said Delbane. He turned to his brother Kings. "Let us sweep this scum away!"

It was Pedrallon who said, "Wait!"

Something in his voice carried enough conviction to make the Islanders listen. They despised him for his physical weakness, but he was still a red Wandsman and a prince, and the old authority was there. He gestured toward the tunnel.

"No one will gain entrance through that gate. Because of the angle of the steps, a ram is almost useless. They may pound till they drop, but the gate will stand. It would be the same for us. I know another way. The way I used when I had occasion to leave the city unseen."

Stark could hear the Iubarians coming up. Between them and the Thyrans, the besieging force could be contained, and possibly defeated. He gave quick orders to the Ironmaster and then spoke to the Kings.

"We follow Pedrallon."

The Islanders snarled. The mob was upon them and they wanted to fight now. In a moment more they would have no choice, and Stark grasped Delbane by the thong of the golden plaque at his throat.

"Do you want this city, or don't you?"

The fierce eyes stabbed at him. The bone knife in the powerful knotted hand lifted. The hounds clamored warning. Stark silenced them. He twisted the thong tighter.

"Do you want this city?"

The knifepoint lowered. "Yes."

Stark turned and motioned on his troop. They began to run—away from the square.

The mob swayed forward, hurling stones, swinging makeshift weapons. They enveloped the Thyrans, who formed square to protect their flanks and rear and began to crunch forward with their shield-wall. The first Iubarian contingent came up, with some of the tall Ssussminh. Within seconds, the square was a floundering confusion as the disciplined ranks began to push the mob back against the pressure of the advancing mercenaries.

Pedrallon led the way swiftly, by streets that were almost deserted now, toward the Refuge, where the Farer girls came to have their babies and give them to the Wandsmen to rear. The windows of the Refuge were full of anxious faces, and there was a great crying and wailing and clashing of shutters as the troop swept by.

Behind the Refuge, and behind the high hostel where Farers who were past their faring could idle out their last years, the wall of the Inner City bent itself around a shoulder of rock. Storage sheds were built against the rock, and at the back of one of them, hidden from any but the knowing eye, was a narrow door.

Pedrallon took them through it into a night-black passage, a rathole where they must tread in single file, Stark and the tall Irnanese doubled forward under a low roof.

"This is madness," Delbane objected, thinking of his men strung out in a long and useless line. "Will the other end be guarded?"

"The hounds will let us know," said Stark. "Just hurry!" And he asked Pedrallon, "Are there more secret ways like this one?"

"Several. Palace intrigues are not unknown among Wandsmen. Also, there are times when the monastic life becomes too boring, and some things are better done unobserved."

There were no side passages, no fear of losing the way. They shuffled forward at a rapid pace, and then came to steps, steep and winding, that slowed them down. The steps went on until all were breathing hard, and it was a relief to find a level stretch again.

"Softly now," Pedrallon warned, and the long line jarred slowly to a halt, all the way back down the stairs and into the lower passage.

Gerd?

Wandsmen. There. Waiting.

Kill!

Somewhere a man screamed.

Pedrallon fumbled quickly in the dark. A strip of light showed, widened, and became an oblong through which Stark ran with his hounds into a huge chamber filled with dusty boxes, dead furniture, and dying Wandsmen with futile weapons in their hands. The chamber contained no more than a dozen of them, more than enough to hold the narrow doorway against any ordinary force. In any case, they could hardly have believed that anyone would come.

The hounds finished their work quickly. Men poured into the chamber in a steady stream.

"We need room," Halk said. "If they come at us now in any force . . ."

Beyond the chamber was a corridor, stretching

away on either hand between rows of doorways. They saw a flickering of robes—blue, green, apprentice gray —where men and boys ran from the intruders or stopped to fight them. But there was only token resistance.

Some of Stark's men were deployed to hold the corridor while the rest of the Islanders caught up. Then the head of his line moved on to a wide doorway, and through that into a cloistered quadrangle where there was more than enough room in which to form their ranks. Wandsmen shouted from the high windows on three sides, and Stark could hear the sounds of the Upper City all around him, stirring and crying like a disturbed aviary.

The cat-footed Islanders formed their companies quickly, rallying to the golden Head. Then they set off again, across the quadrangle and through an arch into a place where three streets came together. All three were narrow, cramped between massive walls. One was short, ending almost at once at the ornate portico of some administrative building. One led steeply downward to the square behind the gate. The third became a flight of steps that swept upward to the Palace of the Twelve.

The square was crowded with Wandsmen, mostly young ones in the lower ranks. A company of mercenaries stood within the gate. From their appearance and accoutrements, they had come from several different troops. Stark could not see how many there were. On the steps of the palace more mercenaries stood on guard, with ranks of Wandsmen behind them.

Stark said to the Four Kings, "There is the gateway to your city. Take it and hold it."

Aud said scornfully, "There is not honor enough there for all of us. What will *you* do?"

"Take the palace."

"Good," said Aud. "Let us go forward."

The mercenaries on the palace steps included a company of bowmen. They commanded the street up which the attackers must move. Aud was for rushing

them at once, but Stark restrained him. Delbane,
Darik, and Astrane were already pelting down the way
to the square. The sharp, clear sounds of strife from
beyond the gate were drowned by sharper, clearer
sounds from within.

Stark said to Aud, "We'll parley first."

He borrowed a shield from one of the Irnanese and
went up the step, his right arm upheld, weaponless.

Halfway up, he stopped and shouted, "There is an
army in the Lower City. There is another one here.
You fight for a lost cause. Lay down your arms."

The captain of the mercenaries answered, "We have
taken gold. We will not betray it."

"You are honorable men," Stark said, "but foolish.
Think."

"We have thought," said the captain, and the arrows
flew.

Stark crouched behind the shield. Barbed heads
thumped on the hard leather. Shafts whistled past him.
No sound came from the Islanders, but one of the
hounds screamed and cries rang out from among the
tribesmen and the Irnanese.

Kill! said Stark to the hounds, and they killed, and
the human wolves behind Aud came up the steps with
such ferocity that they almost overran Stark, who had
taken time to draw his sword.

Another flight of arrows cut into his front ranks, but
those behind simply hurdled the bodies without pausing. There was no third flight. The hounds were angry
and their eyes blazed like evil moons. The mercenaries
fell, and then the Wandsmen; and those who could do
so fled back into the palace.

Stark and the Islanders burst in after them. The
bone-barbed spears rose and fell. Beautiful carpets
and marble walls were stained with blood.

A magnificent staircase rose from the vaulted hall
to the upper floors.

Stark found Pedrallon, and asked, "Where is Ferdias?"

Pedrallon pointed to the staircase. "The apartments of the Lords Protector are above, on the next floor."

"Lead!"

Stark half carried Pedrallon up the stair. The hounds raced ahead and he did not care who followed. But Ashton came, and Halk with his handful from Irnan, and Sabak with his tribesmen, and those of the Islanders who were not still busy.

They found halls of many-colored stone, marvelously fretted and carved; windows of pierced work; doors of carved wood with splendid lintels.

Wandsmen of all ranks tried to defend the halls against these wild, bloody, wayworn men and their terrible hounds. But they had lived so long in an ambience of power—unassailable, unthreatened, adored as demigods by their children—that when the unthinkable happened and these same children came howling at their gates, hungry and betrayed, they had no defenses. They had depended always on mercenaries to do for them what disciplinary work was needed among the providers to keep peace and order. Now even the mercenaries, knowing their power was gone, had turned against them. They were as helpless before the wrath of the lawless as monastic communities have always been, and the proud Wandsmen of the palace died like seals under the spears of the barbarian.

Pedrallon pointed to a massive doorway at the end of a long, painted hall and said, "There."

But Gerd said, *N'Chaka. Wandsman. There!*

"There" was a side corridor, and the likeness of the Wandsman Stark received from Gerd's mind was the likeness of Gelmar, who had once been Chief Wandsman of Skeg.

Think he kill.

Who?

Not person. Thing. Strange thing. Not understand. His mind think: voice that speak, kill.

Stark said to Aud, "I want the Lords Protector alive, you understand that?" Then he was off at a flat run, along the hall, into the branching corridor.

He saw the swirl of a red robe as it vanished through a doorway.

There! said Gerd. *Kill?*

Wait . . .

The door was of dark wood, polished and blackened by the passage of centuries. The metal of the latch was cool and smooth, worn by the touching of countless hands. It worked easily. The door swung inward, into a small room with beautiful linen-fold paneling. A table stood against one wall. On it was an ugly, incongruous black box, defiling with its mass-produced dials and verniers the loving handwork of the wood below and behind it.

Gelmar stood before the box, smashing at the perspex dial covers with the iron pommel of a sword.

"They won't break," Stark told him.

Gelmar dealt the plastic one last vicious blow. "May the gods curse all such matters! And all the men who make them!" He turned the sword on Stark.

Let be, said Stark to the angry hounds.

There was little fencing room in the small chamber, but not much was needed. Gelmar was no skilled swordsman; he only wanted with all his heart to kill. Stark parried his first savage rush, surprised at the man's strength. A sharp clash of blades sounded, and then Stark struck the weapon from Gelmar's hand.

"I will not hold the hounds another time," said Stark.

The dark blood that had been in Gelmar's face drained away, leaving it pale and set, the face of a man who has reached the end of his way and knows it. Yet his voice was perfectly steady when he spoke.

"The transceiver is of no use to you, in any case. Ferdias has already spoken to the ship. It has left us, and will not return."

27

Gerd growled, muttering of lies. But Stark was already reaching for the black box.

"Then why were you so anxious to destroy it?"

Gelmar did not answer.

Aud's Islanders had gone on, but Stark's people had followed him. Now Ashton joined him by the transceiver, as the troops stayed in the hallway, shuffling nervously, awaiting some attack. Soon there began to be terrible sounds not far away. The Northhounds whined, bristling and uneasy.

Wandsmen, N'Chaka.

They did not distinguish individual names, but they knew one Wandsman from another well enough, and they knew Ferdias and the Lords Protector as they knew themselves. Stark understood that these were somewhere close at hand.

There.

"There" was beyond a paneled wall, which showed the outlines of a door.

Stark pointed to it. "Halk. Tuchvar. Take the hounds. I don't trust the Islanders."

"Why so tender of the Lords Protector?" asked Halk.

"They're old men. Besides, Ashton has a use for them."

Halk shrugged and went off through the small door, which revealed a connecting passage. The Irnanese went with him. Tuchvar followed with the hounds, leaving Gerd and Grith, who watched Gelmar with baleful eyes.

The room became very quiet, except for the sounds from the black box, which seemed very loud—and very empty. Only the eternal cross-talk of the universe, having in it nothing of human comfort. Ashton's voice was a monotonous counterpoint as he moved the needle carefully across the shipbands, repeating his name and the emergency code letters, requesting an answer.

There was none.

Gelmar smiled.

Stark asked, "How long ago did you speak to this ship?"

"Three days."

Lies, said Gerd.

"Try again."

Ashton tried again.

The plain of Ged Darod, beyond the walls, held a milling chaos. Where folk had been pouring into the city for weeks, now they poured out of it all at once, dragging wounded, dragging the sick and the old and the very young, dragging burdens of loot. The plain became littered with people and things dropped by the wayside. Streams of folk still incoming along the pilgrim roads collided with the refugees, adding to the chaos as it became apparent that Ged Darod no longer offered any hope.

By the one gate that was solidly held, Sanghalain of Iubar waited with Morn and a guard of Ssussminh. Nearby, the Fallarin also waited, surrounded by the Tarf with their four-handed swords. Alderyk's thin nostrils quivered with disgust at the mingled reeks of unwashed humanity and unlimited filth that the warm breeze brought to him along with the dust and the noise. From time to time he clapped his wings against the breeze, ordering it aside. But the smells did not lessen, nor did the incessant shrieking.

Klatlekt blinked his horny eyelids with the expression of indifference common to his race. His banded torso glistened in the sun. So did the long, broad blade of his sword, which a strong man could not have lifted. He watched the scurryings and cryings on the plain with the incurious contempt he felt for all beings who were not Fallarin.

At length, he saw something in the distance which caused him to raise his round and hairless head even higher. He turned to Alderyk and said, "Lord . . ."

Alderyk looked and saw a great cloud of dust rising on the Wandsmen's Road, coming from the north.

He called Morn and pointed out the cloud. "Get word to Stark, if you can, and warn the Ironmaster and your own captains."

Are these enemies, or are they the allies the wise woman told of?

Alderyk's wings made a small thunderclap. "We'll soon know."

A voice spoke in the room. It was thin against the cracklings and hissings, but it was there.

"Ashton? Simon Ashton? But they told us you were dead."

"Not quite."

"And the other man. Stark."

"Here. They told you I was dead, too."

"Yes. Not more than an hour ago."

Stark glanced at Gelmar, whose face showed nothing. "Ferdias told you that. The Lord Protector."

"Yes. We were forbidden to land, and knowing how touchy the situation is on Skaith . . . Well, with you two gone, we thought we had no reason. We were shifting orbit, preparing to jump. Another twenty minutes and we'd have been gone."

"Hold orbit above Ged Darod," said Ashton, and the sweat was running down his cheeks like tears. He wiped it away. "We're securing the area now. We'll let you know when it's safe to land. Keep open for transmission."

"Understood," the voice said, and was silent.

Ashton turned to his foster-son. They looked at each other, but said nothing. There were no words for what they wanted to say, and in any case they did not need them.

The dustcloud on the Wandsmen's Road halted its forward motion. It bunched up and remained station- ary while the dust settled and the leaders took stock of what was happening at Ged Darod. In a little while, Alderyk's falcon gaze was able to distinguish the blocks of color—dull purple, red, white, green, yellow, and brown—all in the faded leather of the Hooded Men, and beyond them a larger mass of green-gold enclosing dark shapes that perched on tall desert beasts like birds poised for flight.

And now the wings of the Fallarin set up a wild whirlwind that rose high above the plain in dusty greet- ing.

The six old men in white—Gorrel was dead at last and there had not been time to fill his place—sat in the lofty chamber where the casements opened onto the beauty of the temple roofs and the chiming of the bells. Sounds of bitter strife now marred the sweetness of that chiming, and a pall of smoke had dimmed the brightness of Old Sun.

Five red Wandsmen stood by the Lords Protector. The remainder of the Twelve had died defending their lords, and some of the five were wounded. The room and its antechamber were choked with bodies, chiefly in the red robes of high office, but with many others in green and blue and even one in apprentice gray, a boy not yet bearded. It was here that the Wandsmen had made their final stand. Now the naked Islanders kicked the bodies aside to make standing room, and stared with their small, fierce eyes at the men and hounds who held them from further killing.

The hounds grumbled and whined and drooped their great, rough heads. They remembered the mists and snows of Worldheart, where they had served these six old men with their lives.

Pedrallon asked, "Where is Llandric?"

"It was necessary to find your transceiver," said Ferdias. "He did not survive the questioning."

His back was as rigid as ever, his iron composure unshaken, at least on the surface. He regarded the Islanders with disgust. For the others, his bitter loathing was more complex, and for Stark he had a look that was quite indescribable. Nevertheless, he betrayed neither weakness nor fear.

Pedrallon's anger was obvious. "You murdered him. You allowed hundreds of your people to die. And even with your last citadel besieged by your starving children, you sent away the ship that might have brought them help."

"This is a time of change," said Ferdias. "A Second Wandering. Without traitors, we would have survived it. Without traitors, this last citadel of ours would not have fallen. We would have brought peace and order to the world as we did before. A smaller world, it is true, but *our* world, Mother Skaith, untainted by the ways of strangers."

He turned to Stark. "For some reason which is obscure to me, we seem to have lost the favor of her we tried to protect." He paused, and then added simply, "We are ready to die."

"That was in my mind," Stark said, "but Ashton is wiser than I."

Ferdias turned with frosty courtesy to Simon Ashton, who had been his prisoner for months in the Citadel in the High North.

"The Lords Protector will come with us, in the ship," said Ashton. "Nothing else can better prove to the people that a new time has come to Skaith."

"They will know that we have been forced. They will hate the off-worlders even more."

"Not when food and medical supplies begin to arrive. You can plead your cause before the Council at Pax, of course, but I hardly think that the idea of condemning half your population to death rather than letting them emigrate, simply to perpetuate your own rule, will gain you much applause. You can still help your people, by using your special knowledge to help us in organizing the distribution of food and the mass transportation of those peoples who wish to leave Skaith."

Ferdias was amazed. "Surely you do not expect our help!"

"Damn it!" Ashton roared, in sudden fury. "Somebody has got to feed these infants you've created. More than enough of them are going to die anyway, thanks to you."

Unperturbed, Ferdias said, "Suppose that we refuse to go. Will you turn us over to *them?*" He nodded at the sweating Islanders.

"Oh, no," said Stark, smiling. "Not to them. To your own people, Ferdias. To your starving children."

Ferdias inclined his head.

"I take it you're requesting asylum," Ashton said.

Ferdias looked away. And now at last the rigid line of his shoulders had crumpled, just a little. "Our own storehouses are empty," he said. "We gave them all we had. But they would not believe."

28

With the coming of the army from the north, the battle for Ged Darod was soon over. The Islanders held the Upper City, and presently the surviving Wandsmen were joining the fugitive masses on the plain, stripping off their robes and casting away their wands of office, not wishing to be known.

Much of the crowded Lower City was burning, and nothing much could be done about that. Patrols went through the streets that were still passable, rounding up, mopping up. They were assisted in this by the mercenary troops, who had decided to change sides as a simple matter of common sense. Kazimni of Izvand, for once, had more than wounds to show for his trouble, having been among the first with his men at the sacking of the temples.

The patrols overlooked a narrow cul-de-sac beside the Temple of the Dark Goddess, which had been set ablaze by a long-haired girl who sat contemplative in the hot wind of her own creating. The faint traces of body paint were gone from her skin. The bones showed through it, and her hair was matted. Her eyes, like her soul, were now completely empty. Wendor had abandoned her, but that did not greatly disturb her. It was the custom among Farers. She had lost her faith in the immutable power of the Lords Protector. She was unable to imagine a world without them, and she had no wish to live in one.

The Dark Man had destroyed her. She could still see his face, strange and wonderful and frightening. She could still feel his touch. Perhaps Wendor had been right, and she did love him. She did not know. She was very tired. Much too tired to move, even when the flames of the burning temple swept around her.

Within twenty-four hours, the situation on the plain had been stabilized. Most of the able-bodied had fled south, where they had at least a chance of finding food. Those who could not run were gathered into camps under Sanghalain's care. Large bodies of Iubarians and Ssussminh started back for Skeg. Eventually all would return there, to hold the fisheries and control what would once again become a star-port.

The tribesmen and the Fallarin proposed to follow, but Alderyk himself would now lead his delegation to Pax. Morn and the Lady of Iubar would go, as before, with Pedrallon and Sabak and other leaders of the Hooded Men, including one of the last of the Ochar. The Ironmaster, having touched and felt and tasted of the soil of Ged Darod, which was barren of ore, announced that he, too, would look for a new forge-place among the stars.

Reluctantly, Kazimni also volunteered for the ship. Somewhere there might be another Sea of Skorva, where his people could build another Izvand in the clean coldness that kept a man strong.

Tuchvar stroked his hounds. He had grown older and leaner since Stark first found him in the kennels at Yurunna, but he could still weep, and he wept now. "I would go with you, Stark. But I am Houndmaster now. I can't leave them. I'll find a place somewhere, an island, where they can do no harm to anyone, and where they can live out their lives in peace. Perhaps then I can follow you to the stars."

"Of course," said Stark, and knew that he would not. Gerd and Grith pressed close against him. "These two I will take with me, Tuchvar. They would not consent to stay behind." He paused. "Only keep them for me now. I have one more thing to do."

And he left them, protesting, to join Ashton in the

Palace of the Twelve, which was now the Palace of the
Four Kings.

Ashton was speaking again to the captain of the starship. "You may land at your convenience."

"You're on the dark side now. We'll land at dawn."

"We'd appreciate any rations you can spare."

"I've already checked on that. It won't be much, but
it may help. Oh, by the way . . . I think you and Stark
will be pleased to know that Penkawr-Che and his
raiders were intercepted by GU cruisers off the Hercules
Cluster. They put up quite a running fight, but the
cruisers had the weight. Penkawr-Che was among the
casualties."

"Thank you," said Ashton.

Stark was glad, but in a remote way. The weariness
of all the long months on Skaith were superimposed
now on the briefer but more acute weariness of battle
and sleepless hours. The joy of victory was shadowed
by the pain which had never left him since the flames
on Iubar's tower top rose up to warm Old Sun.

He turned to one of the Irnanese who stood guard
over the transceiver.

"Find Halk," he said. "I will wait for him in the
quadrangle."

Lamps burned in the cloisters and the Three Ladies
shone above. There was light enough. The night was
warm. The city was quiet, the air tainted heavily with
smoke from the fires that smoldered below the wall.

Halk came. The hilt of the great sword stood up
over his left shoulder, gleaming.

"I don't see your guardians, Dark Man."

"They're with Tuchvar. They've been ordered not to
harm you, if you kill me."

Halk reached up and stroked the smooth, worn metal
of the hilt. "But what if *you* kill *me,* Dark Man? Who
will gather the people of Irnan together to wait for the
ships?" He brought the blade up out of the sheath,
then thrust it back again with a ringing clash. "I have
much to do. Too much to be risked for the pleasure of

cleaving your head from your body. Besides, I think
you have taken a deeper wound than any I could give
you. I leave you with it."

He turned and strode away across the quadrangle,
into the dark.

The last of the Three Ladies sank in the west. It
was the moonless time when sleep came heaviest, but
Hargoth the Corn-King could not sleep. His people
were camped in the hills above a wide plain whereon a
city was burning. He did not wish to go near the
city, having a distaste for that kind of violence. But
when he cast the finger-bones, the Spring Child pointed
inexorably toward the smoke.

Hargoth felt at once afraid and excited. The blood
quivered within his meager flesh. He stood quite still,
waiting, without knowing what he was waiting for,
knowing only that when it came, much would be
changed forever.

The dark time passed. Old Sun poured forth his
libation of molten brass over the eastern horizon. The
folk of the Towers began to stir, and Hargoth motioned
them to silence. His eyes were fixed upon the sky, pale
and bright behind his mask.

There was first a sound, terrifying, heart-stopping,
magnificent. The brazen sky was torn apart with sound,
and a great shape came dropping down, riding a pillar
of fire with majestic ease. Hammers beat against Hargoth's ears and the ground shook beneath his feet. Then
flame and thunder died and the ship stood tall upon
the plain of Ged Darod, looking even in that moment
of rest as though it merely gathered itself to leap again
toward the stars.

"Up," said Hargoth to his people. "Up and march.
The long wait is over, and the star-roads lie before
us."

He led his people down from the hills, singing the
Hymn of Deliverance.

Stark heard the chanting. He looked toward the long
gray line, and sent word swiftly that there was to be no

attack. While stores were unloaded from the ship and the passengers began to embark—the willing and the unwilling, with Gelmar among the red robes that went to serve the white—Stark went with his two hounds to meet the Corn-King.

"You see?" he said. "I was the true Deliverer, after all. Will you come into the ship?"

"No," said Hargoth. "Until all my people can go, I stay with them. But I will send two of my priests to speak for us." He gestured, and two of the lean, gray men stepped forward. Then he glanced again at Stark. "What of the sun-haired woman?"

"The prophecy you made at Thyra was a true one," Stark said.

He walked back to the ship with the priests beside him and the two hounds at his heels.

Ashton was waiting for him in the airlock. They went together into the ship and the outer hatch clanged shut. In a little while, the flame and thunder shook the air again and set the ground a-tremble. The shining hull sprang upward into the sky.

Old Sun watched it with a dull, uncomprehending eye until it disappeared.